SHOESTRING'S
FINEST HOUR

In the same series

SHOESTRING

Shoestring's Finest Hour

an original novel by

PAUL ABLEMAN

based on the BBC-TV
series created by
ROBERT BANKS STEWART
and RICHARD HARRIS

British Broadcasting Corporation

Published by the
British Broadcasting Corporation
35 Marylebone High Street
London W1M 4AA

ISBN 0 563 17867 1

First published 1980

Printed in England by
Love & Malcomson Ltd, Brighton Road
Redhill Surrey

Chapter 1

I put my ear to the door and listened. Not a sound. I'd already noted that there was no light showing under the door. Was it safe? I had to take that chance. I reached forwards for the door handle and grasped it without making any noise. Slowly, with infinite caution, I turned it and eased the door open. Mercifully, it didn't creak. I knew just were to find what I was after. But would I be caught? The consequences could be serious. I peered into the dark room. As far as I could tell it was empty. It had better be. I started across the floor. It was carpeted but the boards beneath the carpet creaked slightly. I froze. I listened. Not a sound. I took another two steps. This time there were no creaks. I paused again and listened. Safe to continue. I took four light but quick steps. Only the hint of a creak. One more advance and I should have it. I estimated it would take another three steps. I took a deep breath and then took those three steps. Yes! I had it. It was in my grasp ——

The light came on and Erica said:

'Put the whisky down, Eddie.'

'Hm? Whisky? What whisky?'

'That whisky – the whisky in the bottle that you're holding. *My* whisky.'

'I gave you this whisky.'

'Which is what makes it mine, Shoestring.'

'Yes, but – what are you doing here, anyhow? I thought you were asleep.'

'So I was – sound asleep. Until you lurched past my door like a drunken rhino.'

'Lurched? Rubbish. It was my best gumshoe glide. Your trouble is you've got ears like radar.'

'I'm a sound sleeper. But when my water glass starts tap-dancing, I suspect that some creature is stirring and it's definitely not a mouse. Shame on you, Edward Shoestring.'

'Gracious heavens, you don't begrudge me a shot of Scotch, do you?'

'Yes.'

'But ——'

'No buts. Put the whisky back. Better still, hand it to me. It can live under my pillow tonight.'

'I'll come clean with you, Erica. I need a drink.'

'I'm really grateful for your candour, Eddie, and I'll be equally candid. Buy your own.'

'That's just what I did. I picked up a half-bottle on my way home this evening.'

'And you've drunk it?'

'Every drop.'

'Then you've had enough. More than enough. Give me the bottle, Eddie.'

'Yeah but ——'

'The bottle!'

'I have an idea. Let's have a night-cap together.'

'Why are you determined to get drunk, Shoestring?'

'Bloody ratings.'

'What?'

'Bloody ratings fell again last week. That's the third week running. Tell you the truth, love, I'm getting a bit panicky.'

'Yes, I see that your fingers seem frozen to that bottle. Will you give it to me, please!'

'Right. Sorry. I just don't know where it's going to end.'

I sank down onto the sofa and rubbed my brow dramatically. Erica gazed at me thoughtfully. She said: 'I didn't know about the ratings.'

'I didn't want to worry you.'

'Is this just a line, Shoestring? To get a drink out of me?'

'I've got the print-out upstairs. Do you want to see it?'

'Yes. But tomorrow will do. Is that why ——'

'What?'

'I haven't seen much of you lately?'

'Hell no – or maybe yes. I don't know. I guess it must be. I've been too worried to think about much else.'

She came and sat down beside me, still grasping the bottle.

'So, what's going on?'

'Nothing. That's the trouble. No crime. Pilfering and pestering – nothing meaty. I haven't had a good programme all month. I'm pretty good but even I can't make bricks without straw.'

'Do you really want a drink?'

'I really do.'

'Or would you rather come up with me and you can tell me all about it in bed?'

'Both. Tell you about it in bed, with a drink.'

'I just wonder ——'

'What?'

'I'm a fool to wonder.'

'Well, what do you wonder?'

'I wonder which you'd choose if I said you could have either me or the drink?'

I shook my head reproachfully.

'You're not serious? Okay, so I'm not above drowning my sorrows. But to suggest there's any contest. You give me warmth and compassion and tenderness and ——'

'I read you, Shoestring. You'd take the booze.'

'Best of all, you understand me.'

'Oh – get the glasses!'

But when we got upstairs, somehow the bottle remained capped and my sad tale remained unsung. Until the following morning when, over coffee, I told her all about it.

It was a bad scene. Oh, true, Eddie Shoestring, the private ear of Radio West, was still a big pull. My fan mail proved that. But in radio, as in the boxing ring, you're only as good as your last contest. And you can't squeeze a lot of drama and action out of recovering a bad debt or even tracking down a hit-and-run driver who's killed a dog. And those two felonies had been my biggest attractions for the past month.

'There's a station up North,' I informed Erica, 'that's

started a radio auction. People ring up and make bids and the whole thing generates a lot of calories. At least, so Don was saying the other day. I didn't like his tone.'

'Why not?'

'He sounded kind of – hungry. As if it was the best thing since handcuffs.'

'He wouldn't sack you.'

'He'd sack his mother if her ratings fell.'

And it was true. Don Satchley was one of the best programme directors in local radio just because he was ruthless. Oh, we were pals. And we'd remain pals. He'd always stand me a ploughman's lunch and a pint of ale if he saw me begging in the gutter. But if he decided my programme was on the skids, I'd be off the payroll quicker than you could say 'microphone'.

'I've got to love it,' I said pathetically. 'Ouch.'

'Love what? A hangover?'

'The mike – the gleaming, steaming, invincible mike. Remember how nervous I was when I did my first broadcast? How I dried? How I fumbled? How I stumbled? Well now, it's my friend. What was that?'

'What?'

'Didn't you feel it? The house shook.'

'It's your hangover. The house is perfectly quiescent.'

'Really? You have to admit I'm good, Erica.'

'I admit you *were* good. But you just may have entered a downwards spiral.'

'There! You must have felt that one? About ten on the Richter scale. What's a downwards spiral?'

'You worry about your work. You drink to escape your worry. Your work gets worse because you drink. You worry some more because your work is getting worse. That makes you drink more ——'

'Right, right. I get the idea. Do you think this house could be on a downwards spiral too? Why is it tilting like that?'

'You're tilting. Your head's all slumped over.'

'Is it? Ouch. It's better slumped over. Well, what's the next phase? Do I worry some more or drink some more? I don't want to lose the rhythm.'

'You want to get off the spiral.'

'I suppose you're right. How? Give up worrying?'

'Give up drinking! Then your work will improve and you'll be on – well, I never heard of an upwards spiral but I don't see why not.'

'Do I have to spiral everywhere? It's painful enough just sitting still. What gets me – ouch!'

'You shouldn't make violent movements.'

'True, true. Is my head still attached?'

'Why did you thump the table?'

'It just struck me – all the struggle – all the effort – and just when ——'

'Just when what?'

'Well, I pay the rent now, don't I? I'm even saving money. I was beginning to see a bright future – for us.'

'For us?'

'I wouldn't leave you behind, Erica.'

'But where would you take me, Edward?'

'You know – I've talked about it often enough. Shoe-string Investigations – the big slaver's mansion for HQ – the little suite of rooms for you on the top floor ——'

'Of course. I'd forgotten. Your dream. Would it be tact-less to point out that you don't pay the rent very often?'

'It would. No man likes a grasping woman. You earn a very comfortable salary. Could you get me five aspirins?'

'No. No aspirins. They're part of the spiral. Just sit still for one minute.'

I closed my eyes. After what seemed like no time, I gave a loud scream.

'Get up!' snarled Erica.

'Are you mad? Shaking me? In my condition? You might have dislodged my cerebellum.'

'Get up! I've run you a basin of cold water. Go and douse your fat head in that. Then walk briskly round the block. Then douse your head again. And so on until you are cured. I am going to get you off the downwards spiral. I too have a dream, which is getting the rent every week. And, by God,

9

Shoestring, you're going to pull yourself together.'

And, deaf to my pitiable shrieks of agony, she seized my arm and dragged me to the sink.

After about five turns round the block, and as many head-dunks, I actually did feel a trifle better. But I set off for the radio station without any great increase of optimism. What Erica couldn't seem to understand was that just giving up drinking and worrying wasn't enough. I had to have the crimes, the stories, the human dramas, if I was going to win back my ratings. And – unless she was willing to co-operate to the extent of putting on a mask and robbing a bank so that I could bring her to book – there was no way I could create these things on my own. The luck was just running against me.

'Morning, Sweet Star of the West,' I greeted Sonia, the delightful receptionist of Radio West.

'Morning, handsome prince of the frequencies,' she returned absently. 'I've got something for you.'

'Don't tell me. Teenage gang raids sweetshop. Makes off with big haul of Smarties. No? White-haired granny takes up glue-sniffing?'

'It's a girl.'

'What's a girl?'

'On the tape. She's got a problem. She's foreign. Oriental I should say. But she speaks remarkably good English. Perhaps she's a princess from Thailand and she wants you to ——'

'Of course! The big one! She wants me to foil a coup d'état threatening to topple the King, her father, and when I've wiped out the rebels single-handed ——'

'You get her hand in marriage and half the kingdom.'

'Beats a missing child. Let's hear the tape.'

Sonia pulled out the tape on which listeners phone in their little problems. I took it and went along to an empty office and played it. There were three little problems and then a big one. A man had discovered that three tenants in his block of flats were terrorists engaged in making bombs. I sighed. In my first month, perhaps even in my first year at this game, I'd have quivered like a greyhound on the scent. But my nose was more skilful now and it could pick up the smell of paranoia. This was a nut case. It would have to be passed to the police because nut cases can turn nasty and the police didn't have them all on file. But there was nothing in it for Shoestring. I started the tape again and a girl's – no, probably a young woman's – voice said:

'Mr Shoestring? My name is Maria Calderes. I have a problem that I would like to discuss with you. I can't talk about it on the telephone but if you would care to come and see me I think you might be interested. My telephone number is Linksfield 729 and if you will telephone me there, we can arrange to meet. The matter is quite urgent and I hope to hear from you quite soon. I listen to your programme and I enjoy it very much. Please phone.'

I played it again and then I went back to Sonia at the reception desk.

'Sex pot?' I asked her.

This was our not-very-subtle code word for lonely women who ring up famous radio stars like Eddie Shoestring in the hope of getting to sleep with them. It's very unfair of them to do so because it's hell to have to turn them down. But it's either that or back to the dole. There's no way that investigations and sex can be combined. It's not the exploits but the girls that makes James Bond unbelievable. He wouldn't last a week at Radio West.

'What do *you* think?' asked Sonia.

'Could be.'

She shook her head firmly.

'Why not?' I asked.

'Sex pots don't give their name – not usually – not until you ring them.'

'I don't know. That gym mistress gave her name.'

'And her bust measurements if I remember correctly. Still, I'm sure this one's really got a problem.'

'Well, we'll soon see,' I said with a shrug. 'It so happens that I have a little spare capacity this week. I could certainly use a fat, juicy problem. Where's Linksfield?'

'It's about fifteen miles out of town – south-west – near Clavenham.'

'Patch me through – as they say in Hawaii – I'll take it in the office.'

I went back to the office and waited for the phone to ring. A moment later, it did so. I answered it. A male voice said: 'Buttercups.'

'Is that Linksfield 729?'

'Yes, sir.'

'Sorry, I've lost my memo. You're the ——'

'Health farm, sir.'

'Of course, yes. Ah, here it is. It was under my blotter. Now Miss Calderes is —— ?'

'She's the manageress, sir.'

'Right. She's the one I want to speak to.'

'Was it about a booking, sir? I could help you with that.'

'No, it's personal.'

'May I have your name, sir?'

'Certainly. It's – Mason, Titus A. Mason.'

Perhaps it was just the private eye's normal instinct for cover but, without realising why, I'd suddenly decided not to use my own name.

There was a few seconds' pause and then the same soft-spoken male said: 'I'm putting you through now, sir.'

A faint crackle of circuitry and then the voice from the tape said:

'Hello? Miss Calderes here.'

'Hello. Miss Calderes, you left a message for me and ——'

'Wait. I am sorry. Mr *Mason*?'

I said firmly: 'You left a message for me, Miss Calderes, at exactly nine twenty-seven last night. You will appreciate that I have to be discreet.'

There was a pause. She was working things out. Then, dubiously: 'You are phoning from Bristol?'

'Yes. I've received your message. I'd be glad to talk to you about your problem.'

'Well, I think I know who you are. It wasn't necessary – well. I would be very happy to see you, Mr – Mr Mason.

Could you come here? It's less than half an hour's drive.'

'I think I could manage that. When would you like me to come?'

'Oh, very quickly. It is – for *me* – very important. You are very busy, I am sure. You could not come today?'

There was an unmistakable ripple of eagerness in her voice. It was a nice voice, given charm by the faint foreign accent. But Oriental? And Calderes? More Spanish, perhaps.

'As it happens, I am free this afternoon. Shall we say half-past three?'

'Oh, yes! Oh, Mr Sh—— Mr Mason, I am so happy. I look forwards to seeing you. Do you know how to get here?'

'No problem,' I assured her, and then added grandly and unnecessarily, 'I have assistants to plan my routes. See you this afternoon, Miss Calderes.'

But my assistants, which really meant Sonia, had quite a lot of trouble planning my route. Buttercups didn't seem to be listed in any of the directories. The British Medical Association had never heard of it and nor had the Register of Licensed Health Farms. The rates people were cagey and so were the police. In the end, I had to step in and use some pull with a contact at the GPO whom I'd helped with a trivial case. He couldn't give me an address but he gave me rough map co-ordinates and, armed with these, I set off.

Motorways have never appealed to me. It's like driving in a simulator. So I took the A370 out of Bristol and enjoyed the fair new green of a sparkling spring day. I turned off on to a lane at Hewish, slipped across the roaring steel river of the M5, passed through the hamlets of Tealton and then Links-field. I drove another mile. I could see Weston-super-Mare ahead of me and the glittering sea on my right. But where was Buttercups? I drove another mile. No Buttercups. If I went much further, I'd be in a built-up area. Must have missed it. I U-turned and crawled back. Rising woodlands blocked out my view of the sea. I braked. There was a bumpy, unmade-up path, barely suitable for a tractor, winding into the woods. And there was also – no, you couldn't call it a sign but a slanting stake driven into the ground with a ragged bit of board nailed to the top. I stopped the car and got out. I went over to the board. I bent down. Bleached by sun and scoured by wind and rain, a few flakes of paint still clung to the board. I picked out a UTT and a final PS and recognised it as the last mortal remains of BUTTERCUPS. Health farm? If the rest of it was as run down as its sign, it wouldn't do as a convalescent home for dossers.

I looked at the pitted and rock-strewn path and then at my gleaming – well, secondhand but with only twenty-three thou on the clock – Cortina. I couldn't see a happy relationship springing up between them. In fact, a mile or so of that track would reduce my fine chariot to mangled tin. On the other hand, I'd known approach drives several miles long and I was in no mood for a route march. I sighed and went back to the car. I'd take it very easy and, at the first sign of a fatal jolt, I'd abandon ship and hoof it. I started the engine, eased into 'drive' and started to crawl forwards into the wood. The road bent sharply about a hundred yards ahead and by the time I reached the bend I was on the point of bailing out. I'd twice heard the differential clang sharply against flint and my shoulder was sore from having been smashed against the window pillar.

But there was nowhere to turn or pull off the path. Maybe there was some kind of clearing just round the bend. I bounced on, engine growling, for a few more yards, took the turn and braked to a stop. I stopped not because the surface conditions had deteriorated – quite the reverse – but from sheer surprise. Immediately after the turn, and now concealed by the wood, the rude trail was replaced by a smooth, metalled road wide enough for two cars to pass.

'Some kind of initiation test?' I asked myself. 'That first hundred yards must be hell for the sick. Or perhaps they fly the patients in by helicopter.'

I urged my abused car a yard or two further, on to the smooth roadway, picked up speed to about thirty and bowled along for about three-quarters of a mile until the trees suddenly parted and I looked down onto a waving sea of buttercups.

'Christ!' I exclaimed.

But it wasn't the beauty of the prospect, descending in blazing sweeps to the ocean, that had prompted the exclamation. But the fact that, on a small stretch of tarmac beside the grand country house about a quarter of a mile away at the base of the first descending slope, were two helicopters. So they *did* fly them in by helicopter.

I'd heard of discretion, and the passion of the rich for privacy, but this seemed excessive. Surely some of the patrons of the sumptuous place I was approaching – and I could now see paddocks browsed by horses and splendid, landscaped grounds – would come by road. And have to face that first dreadful hundred yards. Mystery here? My sleuth's instincts were aroused.

The road had now broadened into a stately avenue, flanked by lime trees. It wound gently towards the estate, which was sometimes concealed by low, lush hills of buttercup-lit grass and sometimes revealed in closer detail. I'm not really into architecture but this looked to me like a big early Georgian mansion, perhaps originally built by one of the eighteenth-century equivalents of our oil moguls, the slavers. It was in the right area, close enough to Bristol, in the days before choppers, for the man-trader to keep his eye on his business and far enough away for no whiff of the trade's stench to reach him and his newly-rich family.

The avenue opened into a gravelled forecourt, with pilastered terrace above lawns and flower beds, upon which several opulent cars – three Rolls Royces and a Mercedes to be precise – were parked. I slid my Cortina, in which I normally feel pretty smart, but which suddenly seemed as shabby as an off-the-peg suit at Ascot, into the space between two Rolls's, and got out. There was no sign of life – yes, there was. On the small heliport, a mechanic was tinkering with one of the helicopters. I squared my shoulders, to give reassurance against social rather than physical hazards, and strode across the gravel to the front door. This was a massive affair of studded oak but it was chained open and two shining glass doors were the only barrier to access. I pushed through them and found myself in a thickly-carpeted lobby much too small for the proportions of the building. Then I saw that it had been completely transformed inside. The exterior was still that of a grand country house – a stately home – but the interior was that of a smart, modern clinic. There was a young man, immaculately-suited, seated at a reception desk. I wasn't surprised when he addressed me in soft tones.

'Can I help you, sir?'

'I hope so. I telephoned earlier. Mr Mason to see Miss Calderes.'

'Then she's expecting you, sir?'

'I believe so.'

He smiled faintly. He was not an attractive young man. He had wide-set eyes and a narrow chin. The smile gave him the appearance of one of the lesser mantises. But he telephoned through on an internal phone and received the necessary confirmation.

'It's suite nine, sir,' he informed me, 'on the second floor. There's a lift just round the corner.'

He pointed.

'Oh, I think I can drag myself up the stairs,' I said affably, nodding at the ornate sweep of what was obviously the original staircase, doubtless preserved because of its intrinsic splendour but which now seemed out of proportion to the new interior.

I left him and headed for the stairs. Contempt for the soft option was not my sole reason for taking the stairs. I wanted to get the feel of the place. Once on the first floor, and out of sight of the lobby and the young Mantis, I padded swiftly along a carpeted corridor. I passed numbered doors, set far enough apart to suggest that the interiors must be spacious en-suite accommodation, and then came to padded swing doors with glass panels in them. I pushed one of them open tentatively. A private cinema, with revolving armchair seats and individual ash-stands for about twenty viewers. Very luxurious, like Wardour Street at its most showy. But ashtrays? Didn't this health farm know anything about government health warnings?

I went back to the stair head and then mounted to the second floor. A discreet sign indicated the corridor that led to suite nine and others. I followed it. Right at the end was suite nine with a discreet card in a brass frame on the door that proclaimed: 'Manageress—Miss Maria Calderes.' I knocked.

There was rather a long pause. Sex pot, I asked myself, putting the final touches to seductive outfit? When the door was finally opened, the possibility seemed quite likely. The young woman's appearance was certainly seductive. She was dark-haired and had honey-coloured skin, dusted, perhaps, ever so subtly with perfumed powder. Her lips were delicately whitened. Her slanting eyes were surrounded with a hint of green. Her long, slit-sided, tight-clinging gown had a high, clerical neck and was green with a design of fantastic, brilliant-birds woven into its smooth silk. Sonia had been right, at least ethnically. This lady was from the Orient. She looked faintly alarmed, and kept her hand on the door-knob.

'Are you ——?' she asked, not completing the question. I nodded firmly.

'Eddie Shoestring,' I assured her, glancing along the corridor to make certain no one was within earshot. 'But I tend not to shout it. Sometimes helps to sail under a foreign flag.'

She nodded eagerly.

'I know. I listen to your programme. But there was no need – for me. Please come in, Mr Shoestring.'

And she stepped back and pulled the door wide open. I entered a very cosy little sitting-room. It had windows on two sides, through one of which I saw the sea and through the other the heliport. There were two doors in one of the other walls and one in the fourth. The room was furnished with a distinctly Oriental bias, a lot of cane but a lot of cushions too. It held a colour television set, and perhaps five hundred books. The pictures on the wall were photographs of a tropical country, the Philippines I would have guessed. It was a very feminine room, and the only hint of robust

17

amusement was a single bottle of what looked like sherry on a low bamboo-legged table.

'Will you have some sherry?' Maria Calderes asked when I had seated myself on the sofa she had indicated.

'Is it dry?'

'Dry? I don't know. I asked for sherry. Look and see.'

She brought me the bottle. It was a thick, treacly Bristol Cream. I shook my head but she looked so distressed, almost anguished, that I stopped shaking it and said:

'I'll have a small one. I usually stick to scotch.'

Maria smiled brightly.

'It will make a change,' she said optimistically. 'I will have one, too.'

She poured two ample sherries into whisky jiggers and brought me one. Then she sat down opposite me. She was lovely but just losing that iridescent freshness of the girl and turning into a very handsome woman. She smiled, raised her glass and took a sip. I noticed that her hand trembled slightly. Sex pot? Still possible but increasingly unlikely. In any case she seemed to need help to get into gear.

'So you have a problem?' I said encouragingly. She immediately nodded but still said nothing. I continued. 'Well, I'm in the problem business. Do you want to tell me about it?'

'Yes, of course. I ——' she swallowed. 'I have to tell you quite a lot, so that you will understand. Is that all right?'

'That's fine. I have no other appointments this afternoon.'

She smiled quickly but I sensed her mind was on other things. She suddenly said: 'Mr Shoestring, you never say much – on your programme – about your personal life. Are you married?'

I shook my head.

'No. Single. Marriage and detection don't go together. The divorce rate in the CID is terrible. But why did you ask?'

'Only because ——'

And then she blushed. Her skin darkened beneath the powder and she suddenly looked like a native from a jungle village, with fierce eyes and sharp teeth. She stood up and went to the window. She went on, or rather made a new start, with her back to me.

'I come from the Philippines, Mr Shoestring. I came here eight years ago, under a Home Office scheme that allowed Filipino women to come here to do domestic work.'

I was surprised.

'You mean, sweeping up in hospitals and things? There were two Filipino girls in the loony – in the hospital I was at some years ago.'

'Yes, I am like them.'

'You're not. I mean – you're – well, you seem to be a lot more successful than average, to say the least.'

'I've been very lucky. But no, it was not just luck. I worked very hard. I did a course in hotel management. So it was part luck and part very hard work. But, according to the Home Office, I am just a Filipino foreign domestic worker. That's the problem. That is my problem, Mr Shoestring.'

She turned from the window, returned to her seat opposite me and leaned forwards earnestly. I shook my head, mystified, and said: 'I don't really ——'

She cut me off.

'No, you don't understand. Not yet. The problem is that I am Filipino. I have no rights here. I am the manageress of this establishment. I earn quite a lot of money but I am not allowed to have my child. The Home Office will not allow me to have my child with me.'

'Child?'

'Yes. I have a son. In the Philippines. I was only eighteen when he was born. We were very poor. I had to come to England to earn money so that I could send enough home to support my child. But I missed him. That's natural, isn't it, Mr Shoestring?'

'Of course. Of course it is.'

'All mothers want their children with them, don't they?'

'Well – I can think of exceptions but that's the rule, yes.'

'Is it right? Is it right that the Home Office won't let me

have my child here?'

'Why won't they?'

She said very carefully, as if delivering a rehearsed speech:

'When a Filipino worker like me comes over here, she has to sign a form saying that she will not be bringing a child with her. I signed such a form. Now I have a good position and could make a home for my child. I went to the Home Office and asked them if I could now bring my child. They said they would look into the matter. And do you know what they did? They phoned me up a week later and told me that I had made a false declaration on my form and that they were considering deporting me. I know what will happen, Mr Shoestring. It has happened to other Filipino girls. I have read about it in the paper. They will deport me.'

'Have they definitely said so?'

'Not yet. But I feel sure it will happen. It would be a disaster. I love my child, Mr Shoestring.'

'Well, at least you'd see him. You'd be with him. And then perhaps ——'

'No, you don't understand ——'

She was wringing her hands. She went on desperately:

'Please try to understand, Mr Shoestring. Please try to see my great difficulty. If I get deported – can't you see? – there will be no more money. I send money home to support my child. Without it, we would all starve. I must stay here.'

I was sorry for the lady but I was disappointed too. This wasn't much of a case for a radio sleuth. In fact, it wasn't a case for a sleuth at all. More for an ombudsman. If I was completely honest, I suppose I'd have to admit that I was also a little disappointed that she hadn't turned out to be a sex pot after all. An orchard is a pretty thing even if you can't eat the fruit.

I nodded soberly and said: 'Then the real problem is not the child but the deportation. Right?'

She looked at me blankly for a moment and then she too nodded.

'Yes, the deportation. I must stay here.'

I nodded. 'Well, I may be able to help. My programme's got a certain amount of clout. I can broadcast the details and perhaps ——'

But Maria was shaking her head fiercely.

'No! No!' she exclaimed. 'That's stupid. I'm sorry but that is a stupid idea.'

I was a bit stung and said, a little sharply: 'Oh, is it? Well then, what *do* you want from me, Miss Calderes?'

'The Home Office wouldn't listen to you. There is only one way I can stay here. I must get British nationality.'

I nodded. 'That would do it, of course, but how ——'

'I must marry an Englishman. Then – it would be all right.'

I stood up. 'Miss Calderes, I'm afraid I can't see why you've brought me out here. You claim to have heard my programme. Then you should know that I'm a radio private eye not a marriage bureau.'

She said quickly: 'I could marry you.'

It didn't reach me for a moment. Then I blinked and said: 'What?'

'That's why I wanted you to come here – to meet me ——'

'To meet you?' I repeated feebly and then continued, dimly aware that I sounded, in my confusion, like a Victorian lonely hearts advertisement, 'With a view to marriage?'

She rushed on eagerly. 'It would just be technical. I would pay you – anything within reason. And after the wedding, we would never have to meet again. Purely technical marriage.'

Was this a step up or down from an ordinary sex pot?

'But ——' I asked lamely, 'why me? Why have you chosen me?'

'I know you.'

'You ——'

'From your programme. I listen to it. I am a regular listener. I know that you are a good man. Perhaps a rough pearl but a kind-hearted man. Isn't that true? And you have told me that you are not married. And – I have no one else. There is no one else I can turn myself to.'

Her careful English was creaking a bit under the strain. I was touched by her faith in old Whiskyhead Shoestring. But it obviously wasn't on.

'Miss Calderes,' I said humbly. 'It just isn't possible. You must see that.'

'No. I don't see it. Why not? Listen, I wouldn't mind – if you wanted – it would be your right ——'

What could she mean?

'Sorry?'

'If we were married and if you wanted – you would have conjugal rights. I would not deny them to you. And then you could take the money and I would not ask anything more from you – you need not to ever see me again.'

A sex pot with a gold wrapper? A flicker of greed, laced with desire, flashed through me. Then I suppressed it sternly. The lady was obviously desperate. Her ordeal must not be prolonged. I said very firmly:

'Miss Calderes, there is absolutely no possibility of marriage between us. I'm sorry but that's the truth.'

She shrugged nervously. She smiled brightly but the smile wavered a bit at the corners of her mouth.

'All right,' she said, 'thank you for coming here. I am sorry if it – I am sorry ——'

She was crying. She just sat, pretending she wasn't crying, but with monster tears rolling down her cheeks.

I stepped towards her.

'Miss Calderes – Maria ——'

She jumped up and moved quickly away from me. She removed a handkerchief from her sleeve and dabbed her cheeks. She turned to face me, in tight possession of herself again.

'I have to change now. I will be on duty soon. Shall I phone for someone to see you out?'

'I can find my way.'

'Then – please accept my apologies for causing you inconvenience.'

'Listen, would you like me to contact the Home Office?

Just as a friend? Just to see if ——'

'No!' She took a step towards me, almost fiercely. 'I must now ask you to mind your own business, Mr Shoestring. I have made you a proposition. You have refused it. So now the matter is closed. I can look after my own affairs, thank you.'

I nodded.

'Right. Well, I hope things sort themselves out. If you do think of anything I can do, give me a ring.'

She made an effort to smile.

'Thank you.'

'Goodbye.'

I turned and made for the door. I pulled it open. As I passed through I heard an unmistakable sound from behind me. Maria Calderes was sobbing again. I pulled the door shut behind me.

Chapter 2

I felt sad. It seemed there was nothing I could do for Maria Calderes. Worse, there seemed nothing she could do for me. I was no nearer the big one, the all-star spectacular, that would rocket the Shoestring slot back to its rightful place at the top of the ratings.

I decided to take the lift, feeling too disheartened even to tackle the stairs. But, just as I reached the lift doors they slid open and a colourful group emerged. The centre of it was a monstrously fat lady in a wheelchair. She was dark-skinned and hawk-nosed but there all resemblance to a bird of prey ceased. Her cheeks were soft and round. Indeed, her whole face looked as if it had been inflated to capacity by an air pump. She was clad in a green-and-gold sari from which emerged, at the midriff slot, an inner tube of flesh which looked as it if could have supported a juggernaut. Wheeling the chair was the angle-faced youth from the reception desk. In attendance were a nursing sister in regulation blue, two porters heavily laden with suitcases, and a dapper man of about thirty who, judging from the stethoscope in his breast pocket, was probably a doctor. The presumptive client in the wheelchair was muttering constantly under her breath in some exotic tongue and once she reached out, for no apparent reason, and slapped one of the porters on his arm. The nursing sister addressed the receptionist:

'I can take it now, Damien. You'd better get back to the desk.'

The receptionist relinquished the handles of the wheelchair and stepped aside. The nursing sister grasped the handles. The doctor reached down and patted the Indian lady's shoulder and she slapped his hand away. Then the whole cortège trundled away along the corridor in the opposite direction to Maria's suite. The receptionist watched them depart.

'New client?' I asked cheerfully.

I had stepped discreetly to one side and he hadn't noticed me until this point. He nodded.

'The Maharanee of Chandrapore. She owns the third largest collection of jewellery in the world.'

'Doesn't seem to have brought her happiness. What ails her?'

'Obesity.'

'I noticed.'

'She's also insane. If she was poor, she'd be in Rampton. She beat a servant to death.'

'Aren't you being a little indiscreet?'

He looked at me thoughtfully.

'Yes. And it could get worse. I'm leaving at the end of the week. You're Eddie Shoestring, aren't you?'

I sighed. 'That's right – the master of disguise. How did you pierce it?'

'You used to dine at The Trencherman. I was a waiter there.'

'Really? Should think this pays better.'

'If you can stand the stench. I can't. Not any longer.'

'What kind of stench?'

'What kind ——?' His face tensed and his eyes blazed, then he shook his head and the fire died down. 'Different kinds. "Where sin abounded, grace did much more abound." Doesn't seem to apply around here. Anyway, I'm clearing out. I'm going to Bath to work in a hotel.'

'Bath has its share of sin, too, they tell me. Anyhow, if the urge towards indiscretion gets unbearable, you can always reach me at Radio West.'

He looked at me with careful impassivity. Then he stepped back to allow me access to the lift.

'Going down?'

'Thanks,' I said and stepped in.

There was a small, black leather-bound case in the lift. I

picked it up and held it out to him.

'Pigeon-egg rubies?' I suggested.

He took it from me. He didn't smile. He didn't seem a lad with a highly-developed sense of humour. He said, 'I'll have to take it to them. You can see yourself out?'

'I think so.'

He hurried after the Maharanee's party. I pushed the button and descended swiftly to the ground floor. I left the lift and headed towards the swinging glass doors, brooding on what the Mantis – less preying, it began to seem, than praying – had said. But my adventures at Buttercups were not quite over yet. As I reached the swing-doors, a bulky figure in white shorts and vest swung into view from around the side of the building, trotted up to them and collapsed panting against the outer surround. I moved quickly through the doors and grasped him under the arms.

'Are you all right?' I asked.

For a while, he just panted. Then he managed to gasp.

'Kna-knackered.' A few more hungry breaths and he continued: 'Give us – a hand – inside.'

I put one arm round his waist and helped him through the swing doors and on to a brocade-upholstered bench just inside.

He concentrated on the important matter of getting air into his lungs for a minute or so more and then he looked up at me. It was a grey face beneath a grey thatch of wiry hair. It was also a thin face although the body was flabby. It was, finally, a familiar face although I couldn't decide where I had seen it before.

'Jogging,' he explained a little more vigorously. 'First day here. They suggested jogging. Strikes me a cyanide pill'd be quicker and pleasanter.'

'How far have you jogged?'

'Three times round the house.'

'That's not very far.'

'For me, it's a marathon. Next time, I'll get my driver to do it. He's in better condition than I am. Thanks for the helping hand. I can make it to my room now.'

He pushed himself unsteadily to his feet, swaying slightly, raised his hand with feeble jauntiness and tottered away to the lift.

I headed for my Cortina, got in, backed out of the slot between the Rolls's and set off back to Bristol. I noticed there was now a fourth Rolls, half as big again as the others and looking only slightly more opulent than the crown jewels, on the forecourt. I smiled faintly at the thought of the Maharanee, even cushioned by the vehicle's superb suspension, being bounced like a brown blancmange over the brief penitential approach to Buttercups.

There was no point in going back to the station. If anything big, like a kid caught cheating at exams, had broken, Sonia would beam it through to the house. But I did call at the Blackmore Tavern down by the docks. I called there because it was Detective Constable Albert Pelham's favourite boozer. DC Pelham was not strong on intellect, which was why, in his mid-thirties, he was still only a DC. Indeed, he was so thick that if there'd been a rank beneath DC he'd undoubtedly have been demoted. I could never understand why he was kept on in the CID rather than relegated to supervising a police car-park or something appropriate to his mental abilities. I'd once pointed out to Pelham that the Blackmore in Blackmore Tavern was undoubtedly a genteel contraction of the original blackamoor more suited to the local speciality in the days when the pub was built. But it turned out he'd never even heard of the slave trade and after that I stopped any attempt at cultural intercourse with DC Pelham. Then why did I seek out his benighted acquaintance? The police have their snouts outside the force and it behoves the astute private eye to have them inside. DC Pelham had a memory that was about as retentive as a bucket without a bottom but he *had* spent untold years on the scent and had inevitably absorbed a certain amount of information. And, having small sense of discretion and an unappeasable thirst, he could usually be induced to part with any knowledge he had for a pint of Guinness.

'Another pint of Guinness, Albert?' I suggested affably.

'I won't say no,' admitted Albert unnecessarily, since he never did.

I ordered it and then, since subtlety was quite lost on him, asked: 'What do you know about Buttercups?'

He had a way of shrugging his broad face as if trying to shake it into human semblance. He did this now, took a swig of his old pint and then said: 'They're yellow things – plants like. Lot of them growing in the fields this time of year.'

The barman deposited his new white-capped tumbler in front of him and Pelham eyed it appreciatively. I tried again.

'Ever heard of a *place* called Buttercups? A health farm?'

He shrugged his face again and then scratched his chin. He nodded slowly. 'Aye, now that you mention it. Few years back, there was something – I'd have to look it up. Where is this Buttercups?'

'It's near Clavenham, about fifteen miles out of town.'

'That's right,' nodded Pelham, as if some great truth was rising up through the mists of his mind, 'there was something. Can't remember what.'

'Look it up for me, would you, Albert?'

He nodded ponderously again.

'Aye.' Then he added unexpectedly, 'I like wild flowers.'

'Lovely, aren't they? You won't forget – health farm called Buttercups?'

'I won't forget, Eddie. When shall I see you?'

'Oh, tomorrow – next day. No rush.'

'Can I get you another?'

This was just for form's sake. It was clearly understood that the booze flowed from, and not towards, me.

'No thanks, Albert. Have to crack. See you about.'

And I left him gazing speculatively at the froth on his Guinness.

'Evening all,' I carolled, breezing into Erica's living-room. But she wasn't there. I went into her kitchen and made myself a pot of tea. I sat down, lit a cigarette, poured myself a cup and considered the events of the day. Maria Calderes – sad case but nothing for Shoestring. But Buttercups? Even without the praying mantis's dark hints, there was something sinister about the place. The fat, homicidal Maharanee and the exhausted jogger. His grey face, peering up at me, appeared vividly in my mind and another picture – from a newspaper? – lit up beside it. I was just sliding them together when Erica carolled cheerfully: 'Evening all.'

'Damn!' I exclaimed reproachfully. 'I nearly had it.'

'Nearly had what?'

'The name of – Christ!'

'Jesus, I believe.'

'No, I mean – Christ, what are you wandering about like that for?'

'This is *my* house. I can wander about it in any way I choose.'

'I should think any male neighbours might choose the same given half a chance.'

She was wearing nothing.

'They can't see in. The window's too high. Don't be such a prude, Eddie.'

'I'm not a prude. Am I? Maybe I am.'

Erica gave me a speculative look. Then she asked: 'Got a spare cup?'

'Of course. You're not going to drink it like that, are you?'

'Why not? Is this a formal function?'

'What is this?'

'What?'

'You don't normally wander about starkers.'

'I often do things I don't normally do. I had steak tartare for lunch today. First time ever.'

'Why are you naked?'

'Just an impulse. I was upstairs dressing and I'd put on my brassière and I heard you come in and I put on my knickers and then, on impulse, I took everything off again and came down to see you.'

'There's more to this than meets the eye.'

'How could there be?'

'Ha, ha. It's an experiment, isn't it?'

'This is rotten tea. Yes, you're right. It's an experiment.'

'What kind of experiment?'

'I don't know really. An experiment to try and probe the twisted soul of the human male. There is a woman in hospital.'

'A likely tale.'

'There is a woman in hospital who has been beaten to within an inch of her life. The woman is a prostitute. Her boyfriend is a pimp. He beat her up because she was not modest enough for him when he took her to a party. According to him, she was "flashing it about".'

'So?'

'So, what's wrong with men? Why do they always want their own women – even if they're whores – to behave like nuns and every other woman – even if they're nuns – to come on as whores? What ails you?'

'Nothing ails me. Go and get dressed.'

'Macho. You're all the same. Macho.'

'I am not macho. It's just that nude landladies unsettle me. Who is this woman?'

'She's called Freda Manticle, which is rather a beautiful name for a whore, don't you think? The pimp who beat her up is called Ted Richmond or, more commonly, Ted the Slash because's he's got a razor slash on his cheek.'

'Never heard of him.'

'I'm prosecuting him tomorrow. Could do me a spot of good.'

'Small-time pimp?'

'Big-time pimp. But his boss is much, much bigger. Pushes most of the heroin in these parts, name of Willy Clark.'

I gazed at her intently for a moment and then shouted.

'The jogger!'

'Is that an obscure oath?'

'The jogger – the jogger! That's who it was. I knew I

recognised him. Now it's getting interesting. Buttercups.'

'Pansies.'

'No, I'm not playing games. You've connected for me. Here, get dressed. No – no prudery. Get dressed and I'll stand you a dinner. We haven't been to The Trencherman for a long time.'

'Are you serious?'

'Two birds with one stone. Slap-up meal and a spot of investigation.'

And, while she dressed, I told her all about my adventures of the afternoon.

I'd forgotten that The Trencherman was the kind of place where you have to book but happily they'd had a cancellation.

'This is just like old times,' I purred to Erica as we sipped our cocktails in the bar while waiting for our table.

'Yes.'

'Shall I tell you the truth?'

'Don't you always?'

'Yes, of course. I meant shall I confess something to you?'

'Yes, please do.'

'I liked you wandering around naked.'

'Kinky devil – it does seem a pity that men and women can't have mature, candid, sensible relationships.'

'Isn't ours?'

'I admit, I did think so.'

'Nothing's changed.'

'We'll see.'

'Erica, I can assure you – ah, thank you very much.'

The head waiter had arrived to escort us to our table. We dined superbly off mousse de saumon fumé, accompanied by a lightly-chilled Pouilly Fumé, followed by an admirable roast beef en croute with delicate mange-tout peas cheered down by a second-growth Pomerol of an excellent year. At least I did. Erica, afflicted by a touch of the gastric flu that had been coursing round Bristol, restricted herself to a ham salad and mineral water.

'Pricey,' I admitted, contemplating the bill, 'but you'll admit it was more fun than wallpaper.'

Erica's face darkened. Well, most people wouldn't have noticed it but I know her so well.

'What did you say, Shoestring?'

'I know you had your heart set on papering the spare room but it'll keep till next month.'

'You mean you've spent the rent money on this meal?'

'You can't have everything in life.'

She stood up. 'You're not only a pervert, you're a ponce.' And she stormed out.

But I could tell she wasn't really cross. I paid the bill, made a few inquiries about the Mantis, which turned up nothing but the intelligence that he'd been a good worker and left voluntarily, and followed her home. She wasn't really cross but it did take me a quarter of an hour of cooing softly at her bedroom door before she'd admit me. But within another quarter of an hour we were tucked up together and spent a blissful night in each other's arms.

The next day I received a small chunk of a substance that I hadn't seen much of recently: luck. An interesting case turned up on the tape. It took me a week, and in the end I cracked it. It would make a good programme – not great but good. So I was in high spirits when, the final stage of the investigation having taken me out into the country, I set off back to Bristol.

As I sat in my car, I heard a clattering and looked up. I saw a black speck which I recognised as a small chopper. Suddenly, I thought: I wonder if it's going to Buttercups? I checked with a mental map. Yes, my route back to Bristol would take me within a few miles of the establishment. Why not look in? Anything a chopper could do, Shoestring could do – ease up, Eddie. You're getting light-headed. One good programme does not a schedule make. All the more reason for another squint at Buttercups. Something told me there might be ratings in the place. And then there was the forlorn Maria Calderes – I'd been too busy, on an intriguing trail, to give her much thought for the past week but perhaps a visit from Radio West's benevolent Eye might ease her burden a little. How long was it since I'd seen her? About eight days. So the Mantis would no longer be there – if he'd meant what he'd said about leaving at the end of the week. That was okay, too. I could have another shot at playing the man with a hundred faces – well accents – well personalities – Christ!

The exclamation was caused by my head banging painfully against the roof of my plunging Cortina. I'd been so busy with my thoughts that I'd swung on to the stretch of foothills which formed the approach to Buttercups without slowing down sufficiently. As I braked wildly, the car lurched and staggered and I clung to the wheel like a storm-tossed mariner. Then, at a brisk, for that surface, one-and-a-half miles an hour, I danced the hundred yards to the metalled road.

It seemed the chopper hadn't been bearing some ailing Midas to Buttercups because there were now no choppers on the pad. In compensation there were no fewer than seven Rolls Royces, six of them looking like pups clustered round the immense bitch of the Maharanee's astounding machine. As soon as I saw them, and noted that there were no other vehicles of any kind on the gravel, I swung round in a brisk U-turn and eased back up the road a little until I was out of sight of the house. They'd never take me seriously as a prospective client in my four-year-old Cortina. They probably charged more than it was worth for a lettuce leaf and a glass of lemon juice.

Of course, arriving on foot wouldn't do much for the plutocratic image either, so I approached the place by a circuitous route, trying to keep under cover until I was actually on the patio. A small party of men and women on horses passed in the middle-distance as I ambled across the lawn. Do wonders for the horses' waistlines but would it help the riders? So far, apart from the jogging pusher, I hadn't seen much sign of serious health farming in this health farm. I strode up lichened steps on to the patio and made my way to, and through, the swing doors.

There was a girl behind the desk this time. She looked voluptuous and willing. Any way you looked at her, she was a big improvement on the Mantis.

'Good morning,' she cooed.

I selected an accent from a mental pattern-book and tried to match my voice to it. Sounded quite good to me when I said vivaciously: 'And a very good morning to you. Got any rooms?'

Her smile faded somewhat and an appraising look came into her eyes. I didn't feel my clothes would stand up to much appraising so I bounced on cheerfully.

'Only joking. Part of the act. So this is Buttercups? Wally said it was posh but I had no idea.'

'Wally?' she asked dubiously.

'Mate of mine from the smoke. Wally Edso. You must know him. Has a lot of the Mayfair action. He's always up here for a jug of yoghurt and a quick sauna.'

I gave her a suggestive wink.

'Well, actually, I'm quite new ——'

'Don't worry, darling. I won't unwrap you.'

A frosty note entered her voice.

'Did you have an appointment, Mr – Mr ——?'

'Olaffson. My father was Norwegian but the only foreign language I speak is Cockney. Ha, ha. Well, I did speak Cockney but it's got buried a bit under success. I own three casinos in the West End of London.'

'Really?' she said dubiously.

'Check me out. The Sapphire, the Emerald and the Diamond. And the answer to your earlier question is "no". I don't have an appointment. But I do have the beginnings of a paunch. And passing this way, after visiting some old mates in Bristol, I thought I'd give the place the once-over. This *is* a health farm, isn't it?'

'Oh yes.'

'Well, is there any chance of a conducted tour? I could

probably tear myself away from my business interests for a week some time soon and I might spend it here.'

'Well, Mr Cranston isn't in just now.'

'Cranston? Don't recall Wally mentioning ——'

'Mr Cranston is the owner. He's very particular. He insists on – meeting new – new clients – before – before ——'

She was obviously floundering. I pressed my advantage.

'But I'm not a client – not yet. I'm just a prospective client. I don't think Mr Cranston would be very pleased if you turned me away.'

She reached for the telephone.

'I'd better phone Miss Calderes and ——'

'Maria? Maria Calderes? Is she still here? I've met her with Wally many times up West – in the West End of London. They were going steady for a while. No, don't call her now. I'll surprise her. Get some flunky to take me on a quick tour and then I'll have a word with her.'

I could see she was reassured by my knowing Maria Calderes' first name. She smiled.

'All right. I can't see any objection.'

She pressed a button.

'Not that it's important,' I said, 'but what's the damage for a week's stay?'

'Oh, it starts from two thousand.'

'I don't believe it. Wally never mentioned that it was cheap as well as classy. I can't wait to have a shufty. Glad to see you've got a chopper pad. Come in useful if I'm suddenly called back to the smoke to duff up – to attend to business. Hey up, is this the guide?'

The guide in fact proved to be the nursing sister I'd last seen in attendance on the overstuffed Maharanee. I grinned at her rakishly, hoping she wouldn't recognise me. I didn't think she would. She had been pretty harassed and I'd kept discreetly in the background. She gave no sign of recognition.

'What is it, Alice?' she asked, a trifle peevishly.

'Oh!' exclaimed Alice anxiously. 'I didn't expect you, sister. I was trying to get Harry or Martin, to show this gentleman round.'

'They're both busy. Everyone's busy. Oh, I suppose I could spare a quarter of an hour. Are you here for a stay, Mr ——?'

'Olaffson. Not yet, sister, but I'm thinking seriously of it.'

'He's a friend ——' began Alice, causing me to resume hastily.

'All my friends say I'm putting on weight.' I glanced at my watch. 'Fifteen minutes is about my lot, too, sister. I told my pilot to have the plane ready at twelve. So, if you're ready ——'

'Bleep me if anything comes up,' the sister instructed Alice. And then to me, 'I'll show you the accommodation first, Mr Olaffson.'

It was some tour. The place had everything from a rifle range to squash courts. I'd only been round a health farm once before and that was to this like a rubber duck compared to Disneyland. The thing that struck me most forcibly, however, was that there didn't seem to be much emphasis on health. Oh, there were gymnasia and two swimming pools and even a small operating theatre, but the accent was definitely on gracious living. The dining-room, for example, which should have specialised in cold water and rusks, had a menu that would have rocked the chef at The Trencherman. I mentioned this to the sister. She said: 'We cater for all kinds of health, Mr Olaffson. Some of our guests come here to lose weight or tone up. Others for a week of relaxed and enjoyable living. Or you can combine them both.'

'You mean you can eat like a horse *and* lose weight?'

She smiled.

'Hardly. But you can eat and live surprisingly well and still leave a healthier man than you were when you arrived.'

'Sounds like my cup of herbal tea, sister. What sort of people do you get here? I mean, I can see they'd have to have a bob or two but apart from that?'

'We have a very broad-spectrum clientele. One of our guests at present is the Maharanee of Chandrapore.'

'There was a chap in the gym – on the rowing machine – chap with grey hair – I thought I recognised him. Celebrity, is he?'

'Now who would that be? Oh, yes, I think you must mean Mr Clark. He's a Bristol businessman but I don't think he's a celebrity. Of course, we do get quite a lot of celebrities. The Earl of Camberley is one of our regular patrons and Joshua Paul, the film actor. I thought his last film was dreadful but did you ever see ——'

'Holy smoke!' I interrupted rudely, gazing in alarm at my watch. 'I'll have to shift. My pilot gets a bit stroppy if he has to reschedule a take-off. I understand Maria Calderes is still with you? She's an old mate of an old mate if you see what I mean. Perhaps I could just manage two minutes to say hello before I make tracks? Could you show me her quarters, sister?'

'Well – I think I ought to phone ——'

'I haven't time for red tape, sister.'

'I'll take you.'

This was disappointing because I didn't want Maria to give the game away but there seemed no alternative. However, I was in luck. We were half-way along the corridor towards Maria's suite when sister's bleep began bleeping. She said hurriedly: 'I'll have to get to a telephone. Probably the Maharanee again. It's the room at the end. You'll see her name on the door.'

And she bustled away towards the staircase.

Chapter 3

I continued on to the end of the corridor and knocked. This time the door was opened immediately. The reason appeared to be that Maria Calderes was on her way out. She was wearing Western clothes, either no make-up or very subdued make-up, a severe but becoming hat and a light cloth coat. She looked very different from the Eastern enchantress I had last encountered, more mature and severe, but still an attractive woman. Her eyes widened slightly when she saw me but she gave no other sign of surprise. I smiled amiably.

'I didn't come to see you but since I was here I thought I'd look in.'

'Thank you. But you can see, I am going out.'

'Can I give you a lift?'

'No. There is a bus into Bristol.'

'But it's a hell of a walk to the bus-stop.'

'Someone will drive me. We have a lot of cars.'

'Mine's downstairs. I could drive you all the way into Bristol.'

She gazed at me impassively for a moment. The idea didn't seem to attract her. But then she shrugged faintly.

'All right. Thank you.'

When we were in the car, and rolling up towards the woods, she asked me:

'Why did sister call you Mr Olaffson?'

Sister had, unfortunately, been in the lobby as we were leaving and had called goodbye.

'Oh, you know ——' I said, trying to think of a plausible excuse, 'I like to practise, assume different personalities.'

'There is no need at Buttercups. Why did you come back?'

'Always looking for material. Buttercups interests me. Did you know that you've got at least one big-time crook staying there?'

'I am not surprised. Wherever the rich gather there are always some big-time crooks.'

'Doesn't it bother you?'

'Why should it? It is not my business. I am paid to do my job and I do it well.'

'Would Mr Cranston be surprised?'

'No, I don't think the owner would be surprised because I have seen him several times with other big-time crooks.'

'You get a lot of them?'

'No, not a lot. Most of our clients are just spoiled, rich people. But there are always one or two.'

'The police might be interested in that.'

'Then why don't you tell them about it, Mr Shoestring? Frankly, I don't care what you do. I will not be at Buttercups much longer.'

'You're leaving? Hell, you don't mean the Home Office is deporting you?'

'No. They will not be able to deport me now.'

'Really? That's great. Does that mean you've found someone – that you're going to get married?'

'Forgive me, but it's none of your business, Mr Shoestring.'

We bumped crazily across the unmade-up stretch and then turned left towards Bristol. There was a long silence. Then Maria Calderes said apologetically: 'I am sorry. You have been kind. I shouldn't have said that. Yes, I am going to get married. I am going to marry the father of my child.'

I was naturally surprised.

'The father of your child? You mean your child ——'

'Yes. My son is illegitimate.'

She volunteered no more information but my curiosity was aroused.

'But if ——' I began.

'There is a bus stop just ahead, Mr Shoestring. Why don't you drop me there?'

'No, I said I'd take you into Bristol, and I will. But it's

39

understandable that I'm curious, isn't it? I promise, if you want to tell me any more, it'll be off the record. It's not suitable for my programme in any case.'

There was a brief silence and then she said:

'There is very little to tell. My child is illegitimate. I did not see the father for many years and then, a few months ago, I met him by chance. He has been in England for years. He did not look me up. He did not want to know me. So I made no claims on him. Then the – the Home Office threatened to deport me. I invited you to come and see me. You were not interested in my proposal. So I turned to the father of my child. He realised that he had an obligation. He agreed to marry me, to give me British nationality, and I am going now to see him and make the final arrangements.'

'And are you going to – to set up house together?'

She laughed faintly.

'No, Chris – the father of my child – has his own life. It will be a purely technical marriage, as I proposed to you, Mr Shoestring. But it will solve my problem.'

'And once you are married, will you send for your child? From the Philippines?'

'Of course.'

'And is that why you're leaving Buttercups?'

'Yes. I could not have my child with me there. Oh, it will be wonderful, to make a proper home for him at last.'

'I'm really glad.'

'I believe you, Mr Shoestring.'

And then, to my surprise, I felt a slight squeeze on my arm. It was not the squeeze of a sex pot but just an over-flowing of pent-up emotion by a troubled woman towards someone now considered to be a friend. I was grateful. We rolled on in silence for a while, then I said:

'What's Cranston like? I mean, I assume you don't mind my asking since you're leaving soon.'

'I don't mind. Yes, you might get a programme from Buttercups one day. Mr Cranston has been good to me. I owe him a lot. But he has not done it from benevolence but because I was a good manageress. In my opinion, Mr

40

Cranston is another of those big-time crooks.'

'Does he need to be? Buttercups must bring in a pretty penny.'

'Mr Cranston has a castle in Scotland and a castle in France and – they don't have castles in America, do they?'

'Not many.'

'Well, a big estate there. Buttercups does not bring in *that* kind of money. And Mr Cranston is very thick – is that right? – yes, very thick with other big-time crooks. But I don't know anything else. I have been careful not to know too much, if you understand me.'

'I think so.'

And after that, nothing more of any consequence was said until I dropped Maria Calderes at Bristol railway station.

It was half-past twelve. I decided to lunch at The Lightship, which is Radio West's house pub, and then head for the studios and record the story of the successful investigation I'd just completed. As I drove towards The Lightship, I started mentally rehearsing my yarn. I do my programmes in my own words – seize up solid with a script – but I turn things over in my mind a good deal first. Then, when I face the mike, it's like a tap being turned on. The stuff just flows out, smooth as malt whisky which, of course, doesn't come out of any taps I've ever had the luck to encounter. Oh, it's not always quite *that* effortless. I dry sometimes and I've been known to fluff but no one else who rides the waves out of Radio West has such a fluent delivery. And most of them do use scripts. I began organising the words in my mind.

'A good man and a bad father? An irresponsible husband or a highly-responsible human being? A quitter or the chap for the tough jobs? Which one was Walter Burn – er – let's see – Arthur, Edgar, William, Jacob – Jacob's good – Jacob Riley? Sounds Irish. Burnley – that's his real name. Halley? Not bad – off-beat and with a ring of glory. Which one was Jacob Halley? Jacob just vanished one day on his way to work. Happens a lot more often than most people realise. Ask wherever the blue lamp shines and you'll learn how many drop-outs our society ——'

At which point, I pulled into the car park of The Light-ship. I locked the car, entered the pub and stumped upstairs to the lounge bar where they do the best snack food in Bristol. Don Satchley was seated in a window seat with a glass of red wine and a pork salad in front of him. He was flipping through mimeographed sheets. I collected a pint and joined him.

'Good news, Don,' I said, as I seated myself opposite him.

'Not particularly – unless you consider a twenty-three per cent overall increase in studio costs last year to be good news.'

'No, I've got the good news.'

'Really?'

There was no denying it. Although his voice was courte-ous, even unctuous, there was a hint of scepticism in it. Nevertheless, I launched into my account of the pursuit and capture of Walter Burnley.

Don made faint enthusiastic sounds at the high-spots and then suddenly, as I hardly ever did at the mike, I dried.

'Go on, Eddie,' encouraged Don.

'It's junk, isn't it?' I said miserably.

'Not at all. It's fascinating. It'll make an excellent programme.'

'It's a filler. Compared to some of the things I've put out, it's just a holding operation. I've been patting myself on the back but I can see now that it's only because I haven't even had decent fillers for the past few weeks.'

Don took a thoughtful sip of his wine.

'Aren't you eating?' he asked.

'I'll grab a Scotch egg or something in a minute.'

'The Burnley investigation is good, Eddie. It's got a lot of humanity – human interest. But it's short on excitement. You know that. It's not your fault if we don't get our share of sieges and hijackings here in the West Country. And, I admit, the programme, through no fault of yours, is going through a bad patch.'

'Have you got the new ratings?'

'Yes. Not too bad. Very small drop on last time.' Don

smiled pleasantly. 'Eddie, there's such a thing as over-exposure.'

'I don't get exposed. Only my voice.'

The joke was a mistake. Don's steel is only very thinly upholstered. It began to sound through.

'No one's so big they don't benefit from – well, playing a little hard to get sometimes.'

'You want to axe my programme?'

'No, of course not. But it might be an idea to rest it for a season. Invite a flood of indignant letters and then bring you back by irresistible popular demand.'

'Why am I drinking this swill?' I said moodily. 'I should have had a large Scotch.'

'We'd arrange for a retainer, Eddie. You're still the best thing Radio West's got.'

'Which, your tone clearly says, is not saying much. What would you replace me with, Don?'

Don made the kind of strangled sound the prime minister might make if asked: what other problems have you got? He held up his sheaf of mimeographed notes.

'One or two suggestions here: a radio doctor, a radio astrologer, a radio sports coach, a radio yogi, a radio auction ——'

'That's the one, isn't it? You're going to swap me for an old clothes exchange.'

'I'm not going to swap you for anything. I'm just launching a few clay pigeons. Shoot them down.'

'Which of those do you like best?'

'The radio auction has certainly been popular in other regions.'

'But you don't take secondhand programmes, Don. You're the leader. You originate. Isn't that the image of thrusting Don Satchley?'

'The image is expendable, Eddie. The station isn't.'

'I don't think I want that Scotch egg.'

'Eddie ——'

'It's okay, Don. I'll sleep on it. Can we have another chat – more official – say towards the end of the week?'

'Whenever you're ready, old man. This pork salad's admirable. Why don't you have one?'

'You're not eating, Eddie,' said Erica that evening.

'I'm not a glutton for baked beans on toast, then there's another reason.'

'Really?'

'I'm all washed up.'

'What, again?'

'This time it's for keeps. Don's about to sack me.'

'I don't believe it.'

'Falling ratings. No meaty cases. You can't blame him. He's going to run the radio auction instead.'

'What exactly did he say?'

'Oh, you know – sugar-coated the pill. Suggested I take a break. Said I'd come surging back on a wave of popular demand – stuff like that.'

'Well, that's probably what he means.'

'They all say that. Euphemisms – sweet talk. But what it really means is the sack.'

'You know what's wrong with you?'

'I'm a failure.'

'You're a defeatist. One little set back and you want to crawl back into the ——'

'Womb?'

'Bin.'

'I do not. I hated it there. I'd had a genuine nervous breakdown from overwork. Ugh, computers!'

'Well, you're out of computers now.'

'Out of work too.'

'Rubbish. As a matter of fact, I've got a job for you.'

I eyed her mournfully.

'Like what?'

'Like finding out where Mrs Beeston spends her afternoons.'

'Who's Mrs Beeston?'

'Mr Beeston's wife.'

'Erica, this is no time for feeble jests.'

'Mr Beeston is my bank manager. He thinks his wife is having an affair with another man.'

'Could be worse. Could be with another bank manager.'

'What was that about feeble jests?'

'I don't like adultery jobs. They're boring and distasteful.'

'Then perhaps you shouldn't be in the private eye business.'

'I should be ——'

'Yes?'

'I should be ——'

'Well?'

'Appreciated.'

'You big-headed bastard! Don't you get dozens of fan letters every week?'

'Not dozens.'

'Well, I don't get any. Nor do most people. You should be a little more grateful for your colossal good fortune.'

I speared a baked bean and nibbled it listlessly.

'How do you know about Mrs Beeston?'

'Mr Beeston told me.'

'Men don't usually tell strange women about their wives' adultery.'

'I am not a strange woman to Mr Beeston. Thanks to the fact that I am in perpetual financial difficulties with this house – for reasons we won't go into at the moment – Mr Beeston and I spend a good deal of time together. The last time we were discussing my never-shrinking overdraft, which was this morning, I noticed he seemed a little downcast. It didn't take me long to worm the reason out of him. I may say I did so because I scented a possible job for you. And you've got it.'

'I don't want it.'

'Well, you'll damned well take it. Since you haven't got any major investigations on at the moment, you'll take what's going and you'll do it professionally. Do you think I spend all my time on exciting and rewarding cases?'

'Never thought about it.'

'Exactly. You are so self-centred, Eddie Shoestring. Well, if you want to retain my respect ——'

'You mean I've got it?'

'Yes. I think you've done a marvellous job for the past year. But you still need guts.'

'Guts? Didn't I take on those three gorillas from the ——'

'I don't mean physical guts. I mean life guts. I mean not being a quitter. I mean, getting tougher when the going gets harder. You've got an appointment with Mr Beeston at ten-thirty tomorrow at the bank.'

'You know what?'

'What?'

'These beans would slip down easier with a glass of wine.'

'Damn you,' said Erica mildly but she went to the cabinet and brought out a half-empty bottle of cheap plonk.

So that is why I spent all the next day following Mrs Beeston around. Her tastes, as far as I could determine, ran less to silken dalliance than to window-shopping. She window-shopped all morning, had lunch in a hotel restaurant, and then window-shopped some of the afternoon. She made a total of three purchases: two pork chops and a packet of frozen broccoli. When I had watched her safely through her own front door, I went down to the Blackmore Tavern to buy DC Pelham a Guinness.

'Did you find out about Buttercups for me, Albert?' I asked, when he surfaced.

'Aye. It was a horse.'

'What was a horse, Albert?'

'The victim. Six years ago, it were. Someone shot a horse with a machine pistol. Ripped it to bits.'

'Why did they do that, Albert?'

'The theory was that it was someone practising how to use a machine pistol. Never found out who it was. Case was shelved. That's champion Guinness.'

'Could you go another?'

'I wouldn't say no, Eddie.'

'Another Guinness, please,' I instructed the expectant barman. 'Is that all you've got on Buttercups, Albert?'

'That's all. The only funny thing was ——'

But the lure of the fresh pint was too strong. He went under again and when he once more broke surface, foam dripping from his chin, he appeared to have forgotten the topic of conversation.

'The shot horse, Albert,' I prompted gently. 'Buttercups.'

'They found seven guns.'

'Who found seven guns, Albert?'

'Our lads did. They found seven guns on the premises. All of them legal, licensed, and none of them the gun that killed the horse. Will you have another, Eddie?'

'Not this evening, Albert. Got to check out one or two things. Thanks for the info.'

'Any time, Eddie.'

The next day Mrs Beeston only emerged from her front door to walk a Jack Russell terrier round the block and the day after something exceedingly irritating happened. Mrs Beeston got in her car and drove to The Lightship Tavern. There she embarked and drank a sweet sherry. While she was drinking the sweet sherry, a bald man who looked just like a bank manager, and who had been drinking at the bar near to where she was sitting, left. Shortly after, Mrs Beeston left too. I followed her downstairs. She got into her car. I noticed that the bald-headed man was seated in a car parked just ahead of hers. The bald-headed man started his car and drove away. Mrs Beeston started her car and drove after him. I got in my car and started it – and that's when the irritating thing happened.

Someone tapped on my window and when I looked round it was DC Pelham. I glanced ahead. Mrs Beeston's car was disappearing down the street. I waved DC Pelham aside urgently and slipped into gear. But my door was pulled open and DC Pelham said gruffly:

'Just one moment, please, sir.'

'For God's sake, Albert,' I remonstrated, 'I'm tailing someone and they're getting away. I'll see you tonight for a jar, okay?'

'Are you Edward Shoestring?' asked DC Pelham in a

mechanical voice.

'Well, who do you think I am, Tinker Bell? Clear off, Albert!'

I tried to pull the door shut.

'I beg your pardon, sir,' growled DC Pelham and grasped my arm. At that moment, a realisation of at least one of the qualities that endeared DC Pelham to the Criminal Investigation Department became clear to me. He was as strong as a buffalo. My arm felt as if it was being squeezed in a hydraulic vice.

'Let go!' I yelled, more from pain than frustration. 'Have you gone crazy, Albert?'

'The Superintendent would like a word with you, sir.'

I glanced despairingly ahead. Mrs Beeston's grey mini was nowhere to be seen. With the unsolicited help of DC Pelham, I'd blown it. I sighed and, with my free hand, switched off the engine. The numbing grip relaxed.

'All right, Albert,' I said wearily. 'Explain.'

'My instruction, sir, is to request that you accompany me to Bristol Central Police Station.'

'What for?'

'I only know what I've been instructed, sir.'

'I'm not "sir". I'm Eddie, remember?'

'I remember, sir, but this is official.'

'What does the Super want?'

'My instructions ——'

'Oh, drop the PC Plod act, Albert. Off the record.'

'No idea, Eddie. Honest.'

'Funny. I haven't had any contact with Superintendent Bowen – it is Bowen, isn't it?'

'Aye.'

'I haven't seen him for ages. Is it about the nutter?'

'Dunno, Eddie.'

'All right, Albert. Do you want to ride with me or have you got a car?'

'You come with me, Eddie.'

'What and pick up a ticket? I'll follow you if you —— Christ!'

48

The exclamation was a response to DC Pelham once more demonstrating the magnificence of his grip.

'My instructions, sir ——'

'Okay! Ease up before you snap the bone. I don't understand this, Albert. If you don't let go, I can't get out.'

DC Pelham recognised the wisdom of this observation and released me. I got out, none too gratified by the turn of events, and locked up my car. Then I followed Pelham to the unmarked minivan he was using and in which, as far as I could see, he could only resemble a detective constable in an unmarked minivan, and got in. Then we drove in unbroken silence to the cop shop. He knew what it was about. All CID men know about all local CID matters. But he'd been ordered not to say anything. Why? I felt vaguely uneasy. My relations with the police had always been good but they'd never before involved being marched, as it were, in custody to the station house.

I was kept waiting for about a quarter of an hour and then ushered into Superintendent Bowen's glittering office. It glittered from his fishing trophies. If he was feared by criminals he was an absolute terror to pike and trout. He'd caught the most and the biggest of almost everything that flapped a fin.

'Hello, Mr Bowen,' I said cheerfully. 'Any new cups?'

He smiled and shook his head. He was a stocky man with a pudding-basin fringe. He didn't look like either a thief-catcher or a demon fisherman. He looked like the stooge of a stand-up comedian. But he wasn't that at all. I knew some of the things he'd done.

'Sit down, Mr Shoestring. Sorry I had to pull you in.'

'Am I pulled in?'

'Well, I wanted a word with you.'

'Is this official?'

'It's got to be official, hasn't it? I'm on duty. But it's nothing to bother about. Most likely. Do you know a woman called Maria Calderes?'

I thought quickly. The Home Office? They have their own strongarms. Wouldn't use the CID. Then ——

49

'I've met her,' I said non-committally.

'Tell me about it.'

'Tell you about what?'

'About meeting her. Where did you meet her? How long have you known her? That kind of thing?'

'Well ——' I paused. I knew I was up against a man who could read a pause the way a morse-code operator interprets dots and dashes but I was fighting for time. Was Maria in trouble? I liked her. I didn't want to make anything worse for her. I continued, as if searching my memory:

'Let's see, she came to see me ——'

'When?'

'Oh, a couple of weeks back. No, hang on, I've got it wrong. She phoned the station and left a message on the tape. That's right, I went to see her.'

'Where?'

'Oh, the place she works. A health farm called Buttercups.'

'I see. And what did she want to see you about?'

I'd made up my mind. My loyalty, at least at this stage, to Maria was greater than my loyalty to the police. They wouldn't get anything out of me that might harm her position with the immigration people. I told a blatant lie.

'The usual – missing person. A friend of hers – old boy friend, I figured – had stopped answering letters. She wanted to know if I could look for him.'

'And what did you tell her?'

'The circumstances were wrong. It wasn't a local job. I told her it was outside my scope and she should see you people about it. Did she?

Of course I was fishing. But *he* was the fisherman. He ignored my question.

'Was that the only time you saw her?'

'Yes.'

'You never visited Buttercups again?'

'Never.'

I could always admit my little white lie if it became necessary. But I didn't think my antics at Buttercups would go down well with Superintendent Bowen and I was still determined not to give away much about Maria.

'This is an invitation, Mr Shoestring,' said Bowen softly. 'Would you care to come for a little drive with me?'

A cold shiver ran through me. Suddenly my throat felt dry. I nodded.

We went in an unmarked Marina. He was in plain clothes. Just two bluff fishermen out looking for a good stream. So why was my heart hammering the whole way and why did I find my breathing rhythm disturbed? We drove about twelve miles out of Bristol. We ended up in a wood-and clearing about four or five miles from Buttercups. There was a lot of police activity in the clearing. Several cars were parked. White tapes marked out strange patterns amongst the trees. At the centre of it all was the still, cruelly-distorted body of Maria Calderes.

'How?' I asked.

'She's been strangled,' said Bowen.

'Raped?'

'No.'

'Was she killed here?'

'Can't be certain yet but it doesn't look like it. We think she was killed somewhere else and then dumped here. We reckon she's been here about three days and nights. That means she was put here round about, or shortly after, the time you drove her away from Buttercups, Mr Shoestring. As far as we know, you were the last person to see her alive.'

I didn't say anything for a while. I gazed at the thing that had been Maria Calderes. The face was dark and hard and fibrous-looking. She already seemed almost part of the wood. One knee was drawn up. Her skirt was round her waist. You could see her knickers. In a live girl, the posture would have been obscenely inviting. In this dead one it was infinitely pathetic. I felt the shadowy squeeze of her hand on my arm. I saw the fat tears rolling down her cheeks. And now nothing human would ever again issue from this twisted, rotting branch in the forest. I said: 'Shall we go back to your car?'

Without waiting for an answer, I turned and walked back to it. He joined me. After a while, I said:

'Do you think I did it?'

He shook his head.

'No. But you're obviously a suspect. I *would* like to know why you've been lying to me. Shall we go back to town and have another chat?'

'Yes.'

We drove back in silence together to Bristol Central Police Station and there, in the interview room, Superintendent Bowen and I got to know each other pretty well. With short breaks for sips of tea, puffs of smoke and visits to the WC, we conversed for six hours. And it was a conversation – civil, dignified and candid – and not a grilling. Naturally, I did most of the talking but I learned to appreciate what a subtle and perceptive man Superintendent Bowen really was. Interrogation is not easy. It's not like squeezing a tube of toothpaste, the harder you squeeze the more comes out. It's more like restoring a painting that's very ancient and very faded. A good interviewer, like Superintendent Bowen, brings things to light that have been lost, even to the interviewee. He prompts. He follows hints. He speculates intelligently. He pieces things together and finds where parts, which seem quite separate, fit into the overall picture.

I told Superintendent Bowen the whole story this time, of course, concealing nothing – or rather concealing just one trivial thing which I'll tell you about soon – that I knew about Maria Calderes. I told him about her illegitimate child and her problem with the Home Office and the father of her child and how she had bumped into him recently. I told him about my escapade at Buttercups, which he had worked out for himself pretty much already. And then I told him, at his soft invitation, the whole story all over again. And then he suggested we might run over it once more, to make sure nothing had been missed. And it was about halfway through this third rehearsal of my story – when we'd been together about five hours – that I had my great idea.

What astonished me later, thinking back on it, was how

it demonstrated the powers of the human brain. And I don't mean my brain. I mean any human thinking instrument. Because while I went on answering Superintendent Bowen's questions accurately and honestly, concentrating on the subject and searching my memory, another part of my mind was busy organising my audacious plan. I asked Superintendent Bowen about it much later and he agreed that he had noted no change in my manner, that I had been a very good and co-operative interviewee, and that he could never have suspected that most of my mental power was taken up with something quite different from what we were discussing. What was it?

It was: 'The Battle of the Century.' 'Eddie Shoestring Takes on the Bristol CID.' 'Private Eye offers to beat cops at their own game.' 'Sensational real-life detection drama – will suspect private investigator clear his name or will the police nail him?'

That's how it began to flash into my mind in the first place – in headlines. What a programme! What a series of programmes! It might go on for weeks. The listeners would have the nail-biter, the cliff-hanger of the age with their own radio sleuth filing regular reports on his race with the Bristol police department. And he himself was the chief suspect! Don would practically blast-off with delight. The board of management would shower Shoestring with praise and a raise. And my future, when it was all over, would be as solid as anything can be in this fragile world. Fragile – Maria Calderes – one day a warm, worried woman in a strange land and now a dead thing. No, don't think I was callous. I didn't forget Maria. But neither Shoestring nor anyone else could help her now. And part of my determination came from an urge to nail the man who had switched off her life.

While answering Superintendent Bowen's questions, I went on planning the operation in amazing detail. I even considered possible announcements to whet the listeners' appetites. And then suddenly – I remembered something. Oddly enough, although I'd genuinely striven to give every conversation I'd had with Maria verbatim to Bowen, it had escaped me on the first and second rehearsals of my story. It was one word: Chris. Maria Calderes had let it slip – and I'd recognised it at the time as a slip – that the father of her child was called Chris. One of Bowen's delicately probing questions had made it surface in my mind and – I concealed it. Okay, it was unethical. I suppose it was even illegal, since I was withholding evidence. But if I was going to go into battle with the police, who had the computers, and access to Interpol, and helicopters, and snouts, and records and fingerprints and all their terrific apparatus, that one forlorn bit of information might help even things up a bit. After all, I might not have remembered it at all. But, of course, I had. Now I went on answering Superintendent Bowen's questions while conducting a guilty struggle with my conscience. I *should* tell him. But the story! The programme! And I could always tell him later, as if I'd just remembered it. In the end I won – or rather the deceitful part of me won. I kept it to myself. And not long after that, Bowen said: 'I think that'll do for now. Thanks for the co-operation. And – play it straight with us in future, Mr Shoestring.'

'I will, Superintendent. Er ——'

'Yes?'

We were at the door to the interview room now. I turned.

'I liked that girl. And I'm a private investigator. You won't be surprised if I do a bit of investigating myself?'

'No, I won't be surprised. But I won't co-operate, either. And don't get underfoot. I mean that.'

He did, too. He had as much steel beneath the surface as Don but I suspected that his was higher-grade.

'I won't.'

And, shrugging to restore circulation, I paced heavily to my car and drove home.

'I thought we were going to the pictures?' said Erica peevishly, because I was late.

'We're at them.'

'What's that supposed to mean?'

'Main feature. Gripping story of murder and intrigue.

And I'm playing the lead.'

'What are you talking about?'

So I told her the whole story and when I'd finished she said:

'Gosh.'

Chapter 4

'One egg or two?' asked Erica, at about ten the following morning.

'The service is improving around here.'

'You just lie still until it's ready and then I'll call you.'

'Why the heavy maternal bit?'

'Because you deserve it. Because you had an upsetting and exhausting day yesterday. Because you've got a great idea and you're going to need your strength. The only thing is ——'

'Well?'

'To have a race you have to have a race-course, don't you?'

'It is customary, yes.'

'Well, have you got one?'

'How do you mean?'

'I don't see it. There's no distance. The police are simply going to arrest the father of – oh I can't remember the poor girl's name – anyway, the father of her child and commit him for trial. No contest.'

I sighed and got out of bed.

'Stay there,' urged Erica. 'Relax.'

'I have relaxed. I am relaxed. I know. You could be right. But it isn't necessarily going to be like that. Why would he strangle her?'

'The father? Well – suppose he didn't want to marry her?'

'That's not grounds for murder, Erica.'

'All right. They had a row. He's quick-tempered and——'

'And he strangled her? Do you know what strangling someone to death requires? It requires a will and fingers of

56

iron. You have to hang on and hang on and hang on – while they struggle and tear at your arms and your face – Maria was a strong, healthy girl. It wouldn't have been easy.'

'Then you're saying it wasn't the father?'

'I don't know. I'm just saying I can't see any motive for murder. But I can't see why anyone else should have killed her, either. The father is the obvious starting point.'

'And the police will get to him first.'

'Not necessarily. If it really was him, he's not just going to be sitting at home smoking a Filipino cheroot and waiting for them to knock at the door. He's going to be in flight.'

'But the police will at least get a lead on him before you do. Actually, I don't see how you'll be able to get a lead on him at all.'

'I have a friend at the nick.'

'Your Neanderthal DC?'

'Whom you know nothing about. Forget I ever mentioned him. He's just been good for odd tips up to now but he could turn into the key to this whole operation.'

We were both decently clad by now and we went down to the kitchen where Erica busied herself with toast-making and egg-boiling. I sat at the table and tried to plan my operation. Then something occurred to me. I stood up and went to Erica at the cooker. I put my arm round her.

'You haven't asked the classical question,' I said softly.

'What question?'

'Eddie, you didn't kill her, did you?'

'Rot.'

'It's not rot. It's the classical question.'

'Only in sentimental thrillers.'

'We could just be in the midst of a sentimental thriller.'

'You couldn't kill that rabbit that Maisie gave us to make a terrine with.'

'I don't happen to care for rabbit terrine.'

'Yes, you do. You like all fancy food. You just don't like killing things.'

'A rabbit is not a girl.'

'Good heavens, I never thought of that. All right, I'll ask

the classical question. Eddie, you didn't kill her, did you?'

'No, Erica, I didn't.'

'That's what I thought.'

'I could be lying.'

'Oh, shut up. It's in doubtful taste. I know you didn't kill her but something *has* occurred to me ——'

'What?'

'Damn, I've overcooked the eggs.'

'Never mind. I quite like them hard.'

'I could put on some more.'

'Just tell me what's occurred to you.'

'*I* know you didn't kill the girl but aren't you a teeny bit worried about the police? You are the chief – you are the *only* suspect at present.'

'No problem. Bowen wouldn't have let me go if he'd had any doubts. They'll find someone who saw Maria in Bristol or London. My evidence will stand up.'

And I swear it was just about at that point that the door-bell rang. Erica went to it and returned a moment later.

'A Detective Constable Pelham would like a word with you,' she said and winked broadly.

'What? You haven't got any Guinness in the house, have you? He can smell it at three hundred yards.'

Erica lowered her voice.

'Do you think he's brought you a tip?'

'I don't know. I'd better find out.'

I went to the front door, where Pelham's massive frame blocked out all but a faint gleam of the morning light.

'What's up, Albert?' I asked.

'Are you Edward Shoestring ——?'

'Oh, cut the gibberish, Albert. What is it?'

'Superintendent Bowen wants to see you.'

'I've just seen him. I spent all yesterday afternoon with him. Oh, all right, Albert. Let me get my – right, I'll come as I am.'

I turned and called back into the house.

'Just popping down to the cop-shop, darling. Back in a little while.'

And then I accompanied DC Pelham to the trim Honda he was using for disguise on this fine spring day.

Twenty minutes later, I was facing Superintendent Bowen again. Something was wrong, I sensed that. Bowen was tense. He didn't give much away but by now I knew him quite well.

'Anything wrong?' I asked.

'We've checked with the Home Office, Mr Shoestring.'

'Good. And?'

He leaned forward and said: 'Maria Calderes made no application to bring a child into this country. She was not threatened with deportation. The Home Office has had no contact with her for years.'

I was on my feet.

'That's crazy. That's impossible. She wasn't lying. She ——'

And then I stopped. It came in a rush. *I* was lying. At least, that's the way it must look to Bowen. And he now had official support for the view. My tale would seem to him like a cock-and-bull story. Moreover he had information which suggested I was the last person to have seen Maria Calderes alive.

'Sit down, Mr Shoestring,' he said.

I did so, nice and easy. I felt something quite new or at least a different form of something I'd felt on the few occasions I'd faced hard men eager to damage me. It was fear.

Bowen asked: 'Have you ever played American baseball, Mr Shoestring?'

I shook my head.

'You get three strikes and then you're out. You've got two strikes against you now. This time it had better be the truth.'

'All right,' I said. 'I'll tell you the truth. But all I can tell you is what I told you yesterday. Because that was the truth. That's what she told me. She must have been lying. It sounded like the truth to me. I passed it on in good faith. I know you have no reason to believe me but I told you the truth yesterday.'

'We'll take it again from the top.'

We took it again from the top and then again and then again. I was with him three hours this time. And, naturally, he didn't shake me because I *was* telling the truth. At the end, I thought I'd convinced him.

'Are you going to keep me here?' I asked him.

'I'm tempted to. But no – you're not under arrest.'

'I can go?'

'You can go – for now.'

I hesitated.

'Well, go – go, Shoestring, while the going's good.'

'What are you going to do?'

'What I'm *not* going to do is confide in you. And I'm not going to look for the father of that woman's child since she didn't have a child.'

'She might have ——'

'We're checking with the Manila police.'

'That place – Buttercups ——'

He looked up, a shade wearily I thought.

'Yes? That place? Buttercups?'

'It's an up-market thieves' kitchen.'

'That had not escaped our attention, Mr Shoestring.'

'You know about it?'

'It's where the Mafia plan their operations when they're visiting Europe. We've known about it for years.'

'Then ——'

'Oh, grow up. What's the point of closing it down? Better to have your wild beasts in a pen where you can keep an eye on them than prowling about biting citizens, isn't it?'

I nodded in admiration and said: 'I bet you've got it bugged, haven't you?'

'Perhaps you'd like to browse through our confidential files?'

'Sorry, I – if Buttercups ——'

'Leave us to check things out in our pedestrian way, Mr Shoestring.'

'Of course. This has shaken me. I mean – from my point of view ——'

'You don't like being a real suspect, do you?'

'Am I a real suspect?'

'Oh, you are. Now, clear out.'

And I left – pensively.

I drove around Bristol for half an hour, stitching phrases together in my mind. Then I headed for the station.

'Morning, Sonia,' I nodded absently.

She gaped at me.

'What's up with you?'

'Quite a lot. How did you know?'

'The facetious greeting that I've learned to expect and adore – where is it?'

'I don't feel facetious.'

'But nothing's ever quenched the Shoestring bravura before.'

'No. Well, nothing quite like this has ever happened to me before.'

'What's happened?'

'Just keep tuned. I'm going to record the announcement now. Fix me up with a studio wizard, would you? Which studio is free?'

'The small one. There's something quite interesting on the tape ——'

'Is it about Maria Calderes?'

'Your Eastern princess? No. It's a robbery at a shoe shop.'

'It'll have to keep. I'm heading for the small studio now.'

Ten minutes later, Roger Appleyard, my favourite recording engineer, cued me with a pointing finger from behind his sound-proof glass partition and I began:

'This is Eddie Shoestring, reporting from the other side of the tracks. Usually I've been the hunter. Well, now I'm the hunted. What's it all about? Yesterday morning, two hikers found the body of a girl in a woodland clearing some ten miles out of Bristol. She had been strangled. Her name was Maria Calderes. The Bristol police have discovered that the last person to see her alive was one Edward Shoestring, the Private Ear of Radio West. They're wrong because the last person to see Maria Calderes alive was the man who killed her. The police think that Eddie Shoestring and that man might have been one and the same person. So I'm the chief suspect. Well, I'm in the problem-solving business, which does not involve strangling unhappy girls. But I knew Maria Calderes. She came to me with a problem. And the police are perfectly correct in thinking I saw her about the time – but before the time – she met her fate. I drove her from the health farm where she worked into Bristol. But, although there were witnesses who saw us leave the health farm, the police have so far found none who saw us arrive at Bristol. So, fans, this time I'm fighting not only to find the criminal but to clear my own name. And I don't have to tell you what the stakes could be. I don't think any prosecuting barrister could make the charge stick. But innocent men have gone to prison before now. So the regular reports you'll be getting from now on will be reports of Eddie Shoestring's hunt for a murderer and also his efforts to clear his own name. The police are looking for the murderer, too. I say that I'll get to him first. In fact I challenge the police to a race. They've got all the back-up in the world. But I'm more highly-motivated. I want to keep my liberty and, what's more, I liked that girl and I want to get her killer. This is the big one, listeners – the private eye with everything to win – or lose. Keep listening. I'm off to London now on the first stage of my investigation. This flash is recorded but every report from now on will be live. You'll hear it before the police do unless they're sensible enough to tune in, too. Eddie Shoestring signing off.'

I gave the thumbs up to Roger and noticed, with some amusement, that he was goggling at me in quite a satisfying way. Then I left the studio, called at the Gents and then walked upstairs to Don's glass-sided office. I knocked and opened the door. My voice filled his smart, slightly flashy office and Don was on his feet. I'd never actually seen it happen to a human mouth before but his jaw had perceptibly dropped. Appleyard must have been impressed to beam it straight through like this. I hadn't given him instructions to do so. I sat down and listened to the playback. No doubt, it was good stuff.

'Eddie Shoestring signing off,' said the electronic replica of my voice. Don sat down and pressed the 'off' switch on his desk.

'Just a formality,' he said apologetically, 'but I have to ask. Is all that true?'

'As grief. I wouldn't make it up, Don. I haven't flipped yet. And it wouldn't really carry, would it? For long?'

'No, but ——'

'But I was worried about my job? Well, now I'm worried about my freedom, as I said on the tape. Oh, I suppose I was jacking up the pressure a bit for the ears out there but I'm certainly at risk. That girl seems to have lied to me and the police aren't sure that it wasn't me lying to them. It's dicey all right.'

'They're not going to like it,' Don mused.

'Who aren't?'

'The lads in blue. It's obvious, isn't it? You could get in their way, screw up their investigation. They don't like cowboys at any time – but with you a suspect ——'

'Don,' I said reproachfully, 'you're not – you couldn't be saying you're not going to put it out?'

'No, I'm not saying that.'

'You'll transmit it?'

'No ——'

'You bastard!'

'I won't just transmit it. I'll frame it in trumpet fanfares and I'll blast it out, over and over. This could be the biggest thing that's ever happened in local radio. If we're lucky.'

'Lucky?'

'Well, it might be a nine-hour wonder. I mean, they could nail him any minute and prick the whole bubble.'

'They won't.'

'How do you know, Eddie?'

'Because ——' and then I got it, the significance of the curious way Don had asked the question. '*You* don't think I did it?'

'Well? Did you?'

'So it *is* used.'

'What's used?'

'The classic question. The one you've just asked. Do you really think I could have done it?'

Don sighed.

'Christie's boss thought he was an upright chap and for all I know Dr Crippen's patients considered him a saint.'

'But they were both creepy. Am I creepy?'

'No, Eddie, you're not creepy. And if it was a little matter of a bet, I'd lay a hundred pounds at a thousand to one against you being guilty. But for the sake of the station, I have to ask – did you kill the girl?'

'No. But if I had done, would I have said "yes"?'

'Probably not.'

'So what's been gained?'

'I can always tell the board I had your assurance you weren't guilty.'

'God save the board. Now, I'll need unlimited expenses ——'

'Eddie! No one's ever had unlimited expenses at Radio West. If Marconi himself returned to earth and offered to work for us, I wouldn't give him unlimited expenses.'

'Lavish expenses.'

'Reasonable expenses.'

'We won't haggle.'

'We just did.'

'Don, please. I've got things to do. I'm heading for the smoke. I may be gone a day or two. I'll report in as soon as I get back. You'll probably get a lot of calls after you've put out my tape. If there's anything that sounds like a lead, try and keep it for me ——'

'Impossible.'

'I know. You've got to co-operate with the law. But think of the glory for the station if I come in ahead of them. Just bear that in mind. You can schedule my first broadcast for the day after tomorrow although if I come up with something big before then I might do a supplementary. See you, Don.'

'Goodbye, Eddie. Good hunting.'

You know how it is? A phrase you've heard a thousand times suddenly has meaning. Good hunting. That's what people always say to investigators and you get so used to it you don't even hear it. But suddenly it had meaning. I thought about it as I walked to my car. That's why I felt fine. That's why I could feel my body all toned up and ready for any challenge. That's why my mind seemed to be humming like a big dynamo in a power-house. Because I was *hunting*! That's what I was, one of nature's hunters. For years I'd thought I was one of nature's computer programmers. But my basic insinct had won – the instinct of a hunter. Not a good or noble thing to be – the wolf pack baying after the exhausted stag, the faint, infinitely exciting scent beckoning the predator on. And me, Eddie Shoestring, a mild kind of fellow who wouldn't strangle a girl or even a rabbit – but a born hunter. Well, it might not be noble but it used to be necessary. For thousands of years, the human race wouldn't have survived if it couldn't hunt. And I didn't hunt to kill. I hunted killers. And this time I was after the biggest quarry of my life.

Halfway home I switched on the radio and two minutes later there was a flash which shattered poor Marcia Bindweed's Home Handygirl's Slot. No, Don hadn't yet managed to dig a trumpet fanfare out of the library but he did the flash himself, live.

'This is Don Satchley, the programme director of Radio West. Stay tuned because we're about to bring you one of the most remarkable announcements Radio West, or any other station for that matter, has ever put out. All I want to say is that all of us here at the station are behind Eddie Shoestring in his hour of trial. What hour of trial? I'll let Eddie tell you about it.'

Christ, he *had* got trumpets. The fanfare sounded so pretentious I glanced in embarrassment to see if anyone in a passing car was laughing his head off. But there weren't any passing cars.

'This is Eddie Shoestring ——'

Shoestring, the hunter, I thought as I switched off the radio, the hunter whose ghost voice can be endlessly called up and sent pulsing through the air to all you law-abiding citizens of Bristol and district. What was happening in the city? Had pensioners stopped rocking and were sitting with expressions of amazement frozen on their faces? Were salesmen in Cortinas cocking an ear to the dashboard speaker and slowing down, although they had important meetings with managing directors, to concentrate on the dramatic message? Were workers on building sites beckoning their mates to the tranny to listen? Was anyone paying a blind bit of attention or was the background buzz of radio simply coursing through their lives as usual without leaving even a trace of sediment? Who could tell? Well, perhaps we'd be able to tell once the letters started coming in.

I pulled up at the house.

'Did you catch it, Erica?' I asked, finding her at the telephone in her living room.

'Where the hell have you been?' she asked and her tone was decidedly irritable.

'Did you hear my announcement? Just now? On the air?'

'Damn you, Shoestring!'

'Why?' I asked, dampened.

'You went out this morning saying you'd be right back. You went with that thick detective. How do you think I've been feeling? I thought you'd been arrested.'

'God. Sorry, love. Forgot all about it. So much been happening.'

'I should have been at work hours ago.'

'Why weren't you?'

'I've been worried about you. I've been phoning everywhere.'

'The station?'

'No. Why should I have phoned the station? I've been phoning the police. What's going on?'

'Come upstairs. I'll tell you about it while I pack.'

'Pack?'

'Just an overnight bag. I'm off to the smoke.'

And I told her about it while I packed. As I was finishing the instalment we heard a car draw up outside.

'Erica,' I suggested, 'just glance discreetly out of the window and see who the visitor is.'

'It's a panda,' she reported. 'One policeman just getting out.'

'Are there more in the car?'

'Don't think so. Can't quite see.'

'Someone must have heard my spiel and reported it to Bowen. He either wants to give me a wigging or lock me up. Either way, I can't oblige. Get downstairs. Take our visitor into the front room. Close the door after you. You haven't seen me since this morning. Keep him talking while I sneak out.'

'But they'll put out a call to have you picked up.'

'I'll have to chance it. Get cracking, love.'

She shook her head ironically but obeyed. A moment later the doorbell rang. I heard Erica answer and then the sound of voices. And it soon became clear that the plan, like a good many plans devised by saints and sinners, wasn t working. The cop on the motorised beat wasn't going to be lured into the living room. Maybe he'd seen my car outside and was equipped with the licence number. In that case, he'd probably just go out and sit in his panda, keeping his eye on the front door and my car, and radio for back-up and/or instructions. And my block-busting investigation might be nipped in the bud.

I grabbed a set of plain-glass spectacles from my disguise drawer and crept down to the next landing. Then I put on my antipodean accent and called:

'Erica? Are you there?'

I made it sound urgent, almost panicky. She'd be startled and I didn't want her to give the game away so I shouted again quickly: 'It's the guy on the top floor – what's his name? Shoestring? You'd better have a look at him. I think he's still breathing but he doesn't look too good.'

Erica and the uniformed constable came hurrying up the stairs. I stepped forwards boldly, pointing up towards my quarters and saying:

'Just called up to borrow some Nescafé. His door was open. He's lying on the floor.'

Then I reacted as if with astonishment to the constable.

'Hell, mate, that's pretty fast service. How did you get here? Anyhow, do you want me to phone an ambulance?'

'Not yet,' he grunted, as Erica and he pounded past, 'probably nothing. I'll just have a look at him.'

Needless to say, as soon as they were halfway up the attic stairs, I shot like a greyhound down the lower flight, out to my car, into it and away.

But not too far away. It wouldn't take the constable long to realise that he'd been had and to get to his radio. So I drove about half a mile towards the station and then abandoned my trusty Cortina. I walked the rest of the way at a smart pace, bought a ticket to London and got on board the train without further adventure. Ten minutes later I was rolling towards London.

The way I figured it, Bowen would be hopping mad with me but that was all. My broadcast wouldn't have made me loom larger as a suspect. Probably the reverse. So he wasn't going to make a lot of fuss about my little prank. He certainly wouldn't tie up a lot of police power in searching for me. Not at this stage, anyhow. That's the way I figured it. But, as I've readily admitted, I sometimes figured it wrong. I thereupon rose to my feet, went to the end of the car, entered the toilet cubicle and emerged about quarter of an hour later with a few subtle modifications to my appearance which would, I hoped, combine with the plain-glass spectacles to create the appearance of someone who was not Edward Shoestring of Radio West.

Naturally, I returned to a different compartment. There I settled myself comfortably in a corner seat (the train was only about half full) and thought things over.

What had I got? Maria Calderes, a very attractive Filipino girl who was manageress of a top people's health farm that doubled as a crooks' meeting-house, had approached me with a proposal of marriage. She had told me the Home Office wanted to export her because she wanted to import her child from the Philippines. But the Home Office denied this. And there was no conceivable reason for the Home Office to lie. Could they have made a mistake? Well, that was the first thing I had to establish. Continue. Maria Calderes had made no further attempt to contact me. But I had contacted her, more or less casually. She had been on her way out. Going where? To meet 'the father of my child'. She had used that phrase several times. She had meant it. She had even given him a name: Chris, which I had naughtily withheld from the police. But she couldn't have meant it because she didn't have a child. Well, that hadn't been firmly established yet. I had dropped her at Bristol railway station. She was presumably going to meet this mysterious father somewhere out of Bristol. On the other hand, he might have been arriving. She hadn't told me where she was planning to contact Chris but she had admitted that she'd been in touch with him. And she'd bumped into him by chance some months – I think she'd said – before. Could she have been lying? All investigators get a nose for it and I didn't think she had been. I was quite certain that she hadn't been afraid. She'd looked upon her mission as simply tying up loose ends. She had the future planned out. She'd said – and I tensed suddenly. What had she said? She'd said something at about that point which was significant – but what was it? I couldn't quite bring it to mind. I went on with my mental retrospective. We'd parted. And some time, somewhere, in the next few hours, a man – because it was almost inconceivable that a woman would have had the strength even if possessing the will to do such a thing – had put his hands around her throat and strangled her to death. The father of her non-existent child? Why? Or was it something quite separate? Had it nothing to do with Buttercups or the Home Office or children or fathers? But she'd been taken to the place she'd been found at and dumped. She hadn't been driven there by a twisted man, raped and murdered. She hadn't been raped at all. Then robbery? Muggers don't strangle people and dump them in woodland clearings. No, there was a pattern to it, something that *did* involve what she'd told me but which was still hidden.

It was too late for the Home Office when I reached London and I booked in at a hotel in Shaftesbury Avenue which seemed to specialise in dirt, sex and overcharging. As I was woken up for the third time during the night by a giggling couple going past my door, I reflected bitterly that I should have gone to Claridges in spite of Don's strictures about economy. If I was still in London tomorrow night, I vowed, I would go there.

In spite of the amorous hordes trooping through the hotel all night, I proved to be the only breakfaster in the breakfast room. Afterwards, I paid my bill, departed, and headed for Whitehall.

It took me a hell of a lot of talking to get to see Maria Calderes' case officer. I sailed under my own colours. I told them my real name and profession but claimed that I had been retained by her employer to investigate the circumstances of her death. After about an hour of being shunted from watchdog to watchdog, I found myself seated in front of the desk of a grey-haired woman who looked severe but fair, in the best English tradition.

'I assume you've seen the Bristol police?' she asked unceremoniously.

'Oh yes. But they didn't know her. I did. She told me that she'd made an application to you to bring her child over here.'

'That's quite untrue. She made no such application.'

'Are you sure?'

'Yes, I'm quite sure. As a matter of fact, I've been responsible for looking after her ever since she arrived. That's rare because it's been – let's see ――'

She consulted the file spread out in front of her. She continued: 'Yes. Eight years. Usually, these cases get handed on from officer to officer but she was one of my first. So I do know what I'm talking about.'

'Did she have a child?'

'Not as far as we know. These girls are required to sign a

form that they are not bringing a child with them. But we do not inquire if they have children or not.'

'Had she signed such a form?'

'She must have done. Yes, here it is.'

She briefly held out a document for my inspection.

'And you didn't threaten – there was no talk of deportation?'

'Certainly not.'

'But it's common knowledge that it does happen.'

'The position is ambiguous. We are aware of that and we regret it. But in this case, it was never even considered. In fact, we have had no contact with – er – this unfortunate girl since she took her present job. Oh, except for the routine reports.'

'How long was she at the health farm?'

She again shuffled through her slender file.

'She seems to have been employed there for just under six years.'

'Is it common for Filipino girls to be here as long as she was?'

'Oh yes. There's no time limit. Some of them have been here much longer.'

'Could you tell me a bit about her?'

She was silent for a moment. Then she sighed. It was the first sign of humanity she'd displayed.

'I can tell you one thing: I was surprised.'

'Surprised?'

'Yes. It's shocking, of course. But with many of the girls I've processed – well, that's our jargon for it – I wouldn't have been surprised. They were obviously set on finding the quickest path they could to perdition. But Maria was both good and intelligent.'

'But you haven't seen her for years?'

'Just a first impression, for what it's worth. I can't imagine that girl – the one I tried to help – getting herself into any situation that would have led to ——'

She shook her head helplessly.

'Having known her, I feel the same. But she did, didn't

she? How did you try to help her?'

'Oh, I didn't mean anything special – just our usual routine – a job and so forth.'

'And where did you place her?'

She turned to her file again, murmuring: 'I think it was a hotel – yes, here it is. In Bath. The Royal Fountain Hotel.'

'That's a pretty swish place. I know it.'

'I've never been to Bath. But, of course, I knew it was a reputable establishment.'

'What did Maria do at the Royal Fountain?'

The lady shrugged.

'Scrubbed and dusted, I should imagine. These girls came here, knowing they would only get menial employment. It was a lot better than no employment and no social security at home. The Royal Fountain asked us for two general purpose maids, which is undoubtedly their polite term for skivvies.'

'Two?'

'As I recall. Yes, I do recall. It was two.'

'And did you send them two?'

'Yes.'

'Both Filipinos?'

'Of course. That was my job, dealing with Filipino girls.'

'What was the other one like?'

'Oh, good heavens, I'd have to – oh no, I do remember. Yes, now I wouldn't have been surprised if it had happened to her. I can't remember her name offhand but I do recall that she struck me as – well – rather sexy ——'

I repressed a smile at the incongruous word on this spinsterish lady's lips. Oh, I know it's become a respectable piece of vocabulary and that cabinet ministers and parsons utter it cheerfully. But no one yet seems sure whether it's a compliment or an insult.

'Were they friends?' I asked her.

'Oh no. At least, it would have been pure coincidence. They came on separate flights. I just directed them both to the same place.'

'What was her name? The second Filipino girl?'

'Well, I'd have to do some checking ——'

'Never mind. They'll probably remember at the hotel. Right! I think that does it. Unless ——'

'Yes?'

'Is there anything else you can think of? That might be helpful?'

'No. Except what I've already said. Maria Calderes was a good girl. And I would have said an honest one too – until this happened.'

'So would I,' I said with a wry smile. 'Thanks for seeing me.'

I left and headed for Paddington where I took the first available train to Bath. It was lunchtime when I got there and I decided to eat before calling at the hotel. I found a modest, self-service restaurant that seemed to be some kind of community centre as well. It had posters stuck up all over the place advertising concerts and university productions of plays. It was painted in bright pink and green and full of young people who looked like students. But the fare seemed adequate. I queued for a hefty portion of shepherd's pie and a side salad and then looked around the rather crowded room for a free place. The furniture was not conventional restaurant furniture but consisted of rather battered armchairs and sofas. In the far corner, under a flamboyant poster of a bull-fighter, I saw a vacant armchair beside a low table and I made my way to it quickly. I sat down, just registering that the other armchair at the table was occupied by a student engaged in writing his weekly essay or something. I arrayed my food in front of me and took up my knife and fork. The student in the next chair raised his head from the lined notebook on which he had been scrawling and gazed into space. And then I saw that it wasn't a student at all but the Mantis from Buttercups.

'Keeping busy?' I asked cheerfully.

He gave a start and looked at me. At least his eyes did. His mind was clearly light-years away. Then slowly it returned to his body and he blinked and then frowned.

'Shoestring,' he said thickly, 'what are you doing here?'

'Lunching. Like you. Oh, you're not, are you? Just popped in to scribble a masterpiece, have you?'

'Yes,' he said simply. 'I often come here to write.'

'I didn't know that you were a writer.'

'Why should you? I haven't been published much.'

'But you have been published? What's your name? It wouldn't be Chris something, would it?'

'It's Damien Carew-Prendergast. Gustave Carew-Prendergast was my grandfather.'

'Not *the* Gustave Carew-Prendergast?'

As I've remarked before, this was not a specimen endowed with much sense of humour or even, I began to think, much sense of reality.

'The Edwardian poet,' he affirmed. 'The best Edwardian poet.'

'And you've inherited his knack for poetry?'

'It's not a knack. Rubbish. It's hard work. But I'm not writing a poem, no.'

'Novel?'

'It's a – book.'

'Oh, a book? Splendid. So you're not really in the hotel business at all?'

'Yes, I am.'

'I get it. You have to earn a living, right?'

He sounded doubtful.

'Yes – that and other reasons.'

I didn't press him for the other reasons. I didn't really enjoy his company. But this chance meeting might prove useful.

'So you are working here in Bath – at a hotel?'

'I'm an assistant barman.'

'And how do you find the sin in these parts?'

His eyes narrowed.

'You're mocking me,' he said, showing a good deal more insight than I would have credited him with. 'It doesn't matter. I do find sin and decadence and corruption. And that's what I'm writing about.'

'I believe there's a steady market for it. I don't suppose you heard my broadcast?'

'What broadcast?'

'Doesn't really matter.' I paused and then said casually, 'Maria Calderes has been murdered.'

I waited for him to react. It was quite a long wait. Then he repeated, almost without expression: 'Murdered?'

'Yes. Someone strangled her and dumped her in a woodland clearing.'

There was another long pause. Then he swallowed, nodded and said: 'I see.'

'You don't seem very surprised?'

'I'm not. She was a whore.'

'Really? That wasn't my impression.'

'She was a whore. She hardly ever spent a night alone. She was always in and out of men's bedrooms. They were all whores there, whores and evil-doers and scum. It was a sink of iniquity.'

'I think I do agree with you there. Anyone spring to mind as a possible murderer?'

'One or another of her clients – how should I know?'

'You really think she was a fee-taking prostitute?'

'If she wasn't, she was the exception. Wait until my book comes out. Then you'll learn what went on. Do you happen to have the time?'

I glanced at my watch.

'Ten to two.'

He said reproachfully: 'There. Now I'm on duty. And you interrupted my work.'

He rose, clutching his notebook firmly, and prepared to depart.

'What hotel?' I asked him.

'What hotel do you mean?'

'I just wondered what hotel you're doling out the booze at.'

'Is it any of your business?'

I shrugged.

'Not really.'

'It's the Royal Fountain. I have nothing to hide.'

'I'm sure the police will be delighted to hear that.'

'What do you mean, the police?'

'Stands to reason they'll want to interview you. Surprised they haven't already.'

'I haven't been interviewed by any police.' He stared at me blankly. 'Will you tell them where I am?'

'Would you mind?'

He smiled. It made him look as if he'd just spied a plump beetle within tongue-range.

'I don't mind one bit. I am a writer. I have nothing to hide.'

And he turned and scurried away.

I finished my lunch without haste and then followed him to the Royal Fountain Hotel.

Chapter 5

'I'd like to see the manager, please.'

'Have you an appointment?'

'Tell him Eddie Shoestring wishes to speak to him.'

'Are *you* Eddie Shoestring?' asked the pretty girl wonderingly.

'Yes, but I'm in disguise. I'm handsomer than this really.'

She ran her eyes up and down me.

'You'll do,' she said.

'Pray commend me to the manager.'

'What?'

'Sweetheart, I'm on the run. Any minute, you could be raided by hordes of SAS men searching for me. So, please, notify the manager of my presence.'

She rose, turned and disappeared into what was clearly a warren of corridors and offices behind the desk in the imposing lobby of the opulent Royal Fountain Hotel. While she was gone, I wandered about the richly carpeted room and peeked into the bars. There were three of them and in the third I saw the Mantis polishing a glass. I glanced at the desk and the girl was there, gazing at me. I returned to her.

'Mr Wilberforce will see you,' she said prettily.

'How utterly enchanting.'

'What's the matter with you?'

'Nothing. I just like to talk silly sometimes. Take me to your manager.'

She shook her head wonderingly but invited me through a panel she raised in the desk-top and then on through a door, along a corridor and, after a knock, through another door into an airy and commodious office where, behind a nobly-proportioned desk, sat a large, red-faced man with a white quiff. He was dressed in an immaculate chalk-striped black suit and looked somehow like a farmer posing as a hotel manager. He stood up and held out his hand. He said, in an Oxbridge accent: 'Mr Shoestring? I once heard your programme.'

'I hope it didn't spoil your day.'

'Great fun. Great fun. But what time do I get for listening to the radio? But now that I've met you, I'll pick it up again, I promise you. Well now, what can I do for you?'

'You can tell me everything you know, and everything you've got on record, about Maria Calderes.'

'Who's Maria Calderes?'

'The girl that was found murdered the day before yesterday in a wood near Bristol.'

He looked puzzled.

'Yes, I read about that. But why should I be able to tell you anything about her?'

'She worked here for two years, eight years ago.'

'Did she? I had no idea. I've only been here four years myself. You'd better speak to Mrs Crowther.'

'Mrs Crowther?'

'The staff manageress. She's been here – oh, a long time, anyway. I'm sure she'll be able to give you the whole story.'

And she did too. According to Mrs Crowther, two Filipino girls had arrived at the hotel at approximately the same time. They were very different but they became good friends. This was just as well because they shared a room and I got the impression that it was not a very big one. The second girl was called Jean, or at least that was what she was known as to the staff. The main difference between Maria and Jean was in the matter of men. Jean went out a lot and clearly had a lot of boyfriends. Maria worked hard and, when she had finished work, she studied. (I remembered Maria told me she had studied hotel management.) It was no surprise to anyone at the hotel when Jean became pregnant. When her condition became too obvious, she left and that was the last the hotel knew of her. Maria stayed on a few months and then was offered a much better job at a health farm. She left, too, and that was all they knew about her until the tragic news of her death.

'Do you know where Jean went?' I asked Mrs Crowther. She looked doubtful.

'I might have it on file somewhere. She went to live with her husband.'

'Husband?'

'Oh yes, the father of her child' (now where had I heard a phrase like that recently?) 'married her. We were all rather surprised. He was from Devon, I think.'

'So the baby was a – was half Filipino and half English?'

'Must have been. I never saw it.'

She pulled an old address book, with initialled finger sockets, from a drawer through which she had been rummaging.

'I think this is where we put staff forwarding addresses in those days.'

She opened the book and exclaimed:

'Yes, it is. Now, the problem is, what was Jean's last name? I suppose I'll have to go through it page by page.'

'Can I help?'

'No, it's all right.'

Fortunately, she found it on only the fourth page.

'Cole,' she exclaimed in satisfaction. 'That was it. I've put it under her married name.'

'Jean Cole,' I said. 'Doesn't suggest a slant-eyed beauty, does it?'

'Well, she wasn't a beauty. Sexy but no beauty.'

'You're the second person today that said she was sexy.'

'Really?'

'The other was her case officer at the Home Office. May I take the address?'

'Of course. It's in Bristol. Here, can you read it? I'm afraid it's a bit faint by now. I wonder if she'll still be there?'

The address was faint but I had no difficulty copying it. So the trail was leading back to Bristol. Well, that was handy for the station but a bit too handy for Superintendent Bowen and his merry men.

I got back to Bristol about three-thirty that afternoon. I took a taxi to the address Mrs Crowther had given me. It proved to be a small, pleasant semi-detached house in the suburbs. There was a 'For Sale' sign in the well-tended front garden. I went up to the door and rang the bell. It was answered by the sexy Mrs Cole. Well, yes – not my type but, with her ample, rounded bust and rather heavy but sultry features, she might well have seemed sexy to many people. Her eyes flickered over me nervously. She said: 'I know you.'

'Do you? That's disappointing. I'm supposed to be in disguise.'

'Well – I think I know you. Are you Mr Eddie Shoestring?'

'Right in one.'

Her heavy lower lip trembled. She didn't look friendly, but she stepped back and beckoned me into the house. Then she led the way into a small back parlour, neatly furnished and comfortable. There was a football under a piano stool and a puppy sitting on top.

'Please sit down, Mr Shoestring. This is your fault. It is your fault.'

'What's my fault, Mrs Cole?'

'That Maria – sweet, good Maria! – is dead!'

'Why is it my fault?'

'You could have done that – what she asked. It was nothing for you. She would have paid you. She was very generous. Why didn't you do it? Why?'

'You mean – marry her?'

'Of course I mean that. She was desperate. Couldn't you see that she was desperate?'

'As a matter of fact, I couldn't. Worried, yes. But not desperate. How did you know she suggested that I marry her?'

'She was my friend.'

'It's six years since you worked together.'

'She was still my friend. She visited me sometimes. She made much confidence in me. It was such a little thing.'

'You think marriage is a little thing?'

'Compared to her life.'

'I didn't compare it to her life. I didn't know she was going to be murdered. Did you?'

'What are you saying?'

'What makes you think her death had anything to do with me not marrying her?'

'Because she was so desperate. She wanted her child with her.'

'I know. Did you know her child?'

'Me? No. How should I know him? But she talked about him – she talked many times about him – how she would like to make a home for him.'

'When did you last see her?'

The Filipino girl shook her head vaguely.

'I don't know. Two weeks – three weeks ——'

'She came here?'

'Yes, she came here many times. She liked to see Johnny.'

'Johnny?'

'My child – my son. Because she did not have her own child, she liked to see mine. They were friends. I have not told him – what has happened. If he comes in, you must not tell him.'

'Where is Johnny?'

She got up and went to the window. She beckoned me. I joined her.

On the small lawn, three children were playing, two little boys and a little girl. One of the little boys was clearly part Oriental. He was an attractive lad, slim and tall for – yes, he must be six.

'That is my Johnny,' she said.

'Fine boy,' I said. 'Is his father here?'

She stared at me.

'His father?'

'Yes. Mr Cole – presumably.'

'Willy Cole?' she laughed. 'Willy Cole?' She laughed heartily. Then she shook her head, wiped her eyes and said: 'I have not seen Willy Cole for five years.'

'Oh?'

Her mouth curled into an expression of disgust.

'He was a – drunken pig. He was no good. He just left.'

'Does he support you and the child?'

'Does he support me ——? You don't know what a ridiculous question that is.'

'This is a nice house.'

'I support me – and Johnny. I get some money from the government and I – I do some moonlighting.'

Yes, I thought, and I can guess what kind.

'Listen,' I said. 'You liked Maria. I liked her, too. Have you any ideas as to why she was killed? Or who killed her?'

She sighed and walked to a cabinet at the side of the room. She opened a door in its front and removed a bottle of gin.

'Would you like a drink, Mr Shoestring?' she asked.

I shook my head.

She poured herself a substantial amount and then returned to the window where I was still standing. She took a swig. She said: 'I don't know who killed Maria. If I did, I would tell you. I would do anything to help get the man.'

'Could it have been the father of her child?'

She looked startled.

'What? What do you mean?'

'She told me that she was on her way to meet the father of her child. Who was that?'

'Who was that? How do I know? Some village boy. Who else? Maria came from a village but I came from Manila. I was a town girl. She was a village girl.'

'So you didn't know him? You never met him?'

'No, I never met him. Never. He must be in the Philippines.'

'She said she had seen him. That he was here.'

'No, I don't believe it. She never told me this. I don't believe it.'

'All right. Well, I'm grateful for your help. If you do think of anything, you can always telephone the radio station.'

I moved towards the door. She followed me. She opened

the front door for me. I pointed to the sign and said: 'I see you're selling the house.'

'Yes.'

'Where will you live?'

'In Missississ – in Mississp ——'

'Mississippi?'

'I must learn to say it. I practise and practise. Yes, in – that place. It is a state in the America.'

'I know. What takes you there?'

She shrugged and tossed her head slightly.

'There is a man. I met him here. He wants me to go there.'

'I see. And you'll take Johnny?'

'Of course I will take Johnny. What else would I do with him?'

'Are you going soon?'

'I have to sell the house. I don't know.'

'Well, good luck.'

And I made my way back into the centre of Bristol. I couldn't go home. There might be a police watch on the house. So I went to the Carlton Hotel, a pleasant two-star establishment overlooking the Green. I booked a single room and bath for the night and signed the register in the name of Thomas Becket. The uniformed hotel clerk, a young man of about twenty-five with pleasant, fresh features, looked at my signature, glanced from side to side as if to make sure we couldn't be overheard, leaned forwards and whispered: 'You're Eddie Shoestring, aren't you?'

I sighed.

'Doesn't anyone know the meaning of disguise any more?'

'I thought I recognised you. I saw you on television.'

'But I've only been on television once. It was a thirty-second slot after I'd brought a blackmailer to book.'

'That's right. That's when I saw you.'

'But the glasses?' I asked sadly. 'The false sideburns? The darkened complexion? Don't they make any difference?'

He studied my features carefully.

'Not really.'

'Well, what are you going to do? Hand me over to the fuzz?'

'No. Do they want you?'

'I'm not sure.'

'Well, I'm on your side. That's what I wanted to tell you. I heard your announcement. I believe you should have a chance to clear your name. You can count on my support.'

'I'm delighted to hear it. For the time being, the best support you can give me is not mentioning to anyone – and I mean anyone – that I'm staying here.'

'Right. I won't. If there's anything I can do to help, just phone down and ask for Ferdinand.'

'I will. Thanks, Ferdinand.'

'Ferdy to my friends.'

'Amongst whom you can number me. See you, Ferdy.'

I went up to my room. It had no television but then I had no plans for watching television. It did have a telephone and that instrument I had designs on. I phoned the station and, after ascertaining that there had been many messages of sympathy but no likely leads, made certain arrangements for later in the evening. Then I went into the bathroom and spent a quarter of an hour refurbishing my disguise. Then I left the hotel, winking at Ferdinand as I departed, and made my way by a discreet route down to the Blackmore Tavern. There I sidled up to Detective Constable Albert Pelham who was moodily licking his lips. He glanced round and said: 'Hello, Eddie. The tash suits you. You should grow one.'

I sighed, peeled the uncomfortable thing off and said: 'Can I get you a Guinness, Albert?'

'I wouldn't normally refuse, Eddie, but I haven't got time just now.'

'Why's that, Albert?'

'Because,' explained Albert, as his hand shot out and grasped my arm in the familiar numbing grip, 'I have to get you down to HQ. The Super wants to see you.'

'I thought he might, Albert. But if you'd stop turning my arm into bonemeal, I have a proposition for you.'

84

'You won't make a run for it, Eddie? I hate foot chases.'

'My word of honour, Albert.'

He released my arm and, rubbing it briskly to restore the circulation, I suggested:

'Why don't you sit down over there by the window, Albert, while I get you a frothing pint? Then we can have a nice discreet chat.'

'Okay, Eddie.'

He lumbered off to the secluded table and I bought him a Guinness and myself a large Scotch. Then I joined him.

'I'll put it in a nutshell, Albert. I will buy you, and have delivered to your home, a barrel of Guinness if you will keep me informed about the police investigation on Maria Calderes.'

He brooded on this munificent offer for a while and then said heavily:

'I don't see how I can.'

'Why not?'

'Well, I'm not a bent copper. I never have been.'

'You, Albert? It's because you're incorruptible that I'm asking you.'

'Is it?'

'Of course. You wouldn't betray a friend. How long have we been friends, Albert?'

'Two years.'

'Two long, happy years which have produced unforgettable memories for us both.'

'We've had a few jars together but ———'

'Albert, I'm in trouble. Your people need a suspect and I'm Johnny-on-the-spot. Well, I didn't do it. You know that. You know your old pal, Eddie Shoestring, isn't a murderer.'

Albert shrugged: 'I'd like to help you, Eddie ———'

'That's the spirit, Albert. What about the child?'

'Child?'

'Did Maria Calderes have a child? What did the Manila police say?'

'Yes, she did.'

I was astonished.

'She *did*?'

'Aye, but it died seven years ago when it was still a baby.'

'And she only had the one?'

'Unless she's had another since she's been here. But if she has, we've found no trace of it.'

'Thanks, Albert. That's all I need for the time being.' I rose to my feet. 'Now I'll get that barrel of Guinness sent round – Christ!'

My arm was once more secured.

'Hang on, Eddie. I'd get some credit for bringing you in.'

'Let go of my arm, Albert. I won't make a run for it. There'll be no hot pursuit.'

He released my persecuted limb again. I thought about what he'd said.

'All right, Albert, you can bring me in. But not now.'

And I sat down again and made certain arrangements with him.

Then I made my way, again as discreetly as I could manage, back to the hotel. Once in my room, I phoned down to the desk.

'Is that Ferdinand?'

'Yes.'

'Mr Becket here. A Mr Appleyard will be calling to see me shortly. He'll ask for Mr Becket. It's all right to sent him up.'

'Right you are, Mr Becket. You can count on me.'

Then I sat down in the single armchair and the stresses of the day caught up with me. I went to sleep.

'Ready for levels, Eddie,' said Roger Appleyard, shaking me gently.

I opened my eyes.

'Roger. How did you get in?'

'I knocked and the door opened slightly. Your security is weak.'

'As far as I know, only the Bristol police are on my trail. And they don't use hit men. Why didn't you wake me?'

'You looked peaceful.'

And he handed me the mike. I spoke into it.

'Eddie Shoestring here. Testing, testing, one, two, three-four, five, the quick brown cop jumped over the lazy sleep,ing crook. Now is the time for all good malefactors to——'

'Okay, Eddie,' said Roger, adjusting a dial. 'Take it when you're ready.'

I was still somnolent. I shrugged the way Albert Pelham did to see if it helped and it did slightly. Then I took a deep breath and began.

'Hello, friends and other listeners. This is Eddie Shoe-string bringing you the first of his promised reports on the case of Maria Calderes. First an apology. When I trailed this series two days ago I told you you'd be hearing from me live. Well, I can't keep that promise. Why not? Because I'm on the run, not from the bad guys but from the good ones. The police are trying to pull me in. I've had two narrow escapes from them already. I don't know what they want with me. But if they lock me up, I can't go on investigating and that means you don't get your programmes and I don't get a chance to clear my name. So, listeners, this is what I want you to do. Phone and write to the police at Bristol Central telling them you support me and my quest. Put the word around. Hands off Eddie Shoestring. Let him do his job. You all know that I've pulled off a few big strokes in the past and nailed some villains that have slipped through Old Bill's hands. And this time, the stakes are very high. For me. So let them know you're supporting me. I'm recording this tape at a secret location but don't worry – you'll get it very soon. As soon as I've finished, it will be rushed to the studio and sent out. I reckon you'll be hearing it not more than twenty minutes after I've spoken the last word. Now this is where it's at. Nothing dramatic so far – just the results of my preliminary investigations. I've been clearing the ground and I'm getting ready to take off . . .'

Then I gave them a succinct account of my movements and meetings of the past couple of days, trying to build as much drama and comedy into it as I could but aware that the material was not intrinsically all that exciting. Still, it *was* a murder investigation and all those millions out there were sharing it with me. And I was pretty confident that my ending would keep them coming back for more.

'. . . So the signs point East. Maria Calderes was on her way to meet the "father of her child" when she met her doom. He was going to marry her so that she could avoid deportation. But she hadn't been threatened with deportation. Did she have a child? Yes, but it died while still a baby. But her best friend thought she still had one. Somewhere, over there, in the distant Philippines, must be the clue that will help resolve these contradictions. So that's where Eddie Shoestring is going. The next time you hear from me, I'll have just stepped off a jumbo and I hope to bring you at least part of the answer to this puzzle. Back me up. Let the police know that you're behind me. And keep your fingers crossed. Shoestring signing off.'

Roger flipped some switches and back it came at me, some of the sentences I'd just spoken. The miracle of modern electronic communications remains a miracle to me. A lot of magnetic particles on a stretch of plastic tape turn into the living (you'd swear) voice of Eddie Shoestring or anyone else.

'How'd it sound, Roger?' I asked, when silence reigned once more.

'It's a winner, Eddie. If you pull it off you'll be able to write your own pay-cheques.'

'But would Don sign them? Anyway, what do I want with money? A spot of caviar and champagne at weekends and a mansion I've set my heart on – I'm a fellow of simple tastes.'

Roger grinned as he packed up his equipment. I said: 'I don't think anyone's grassed on me, Roger, but keep an eye out as you leave the hotel. I want this one to hit the air.'

He gave me the thumbs-up sign, hoisted his heavy machine and departed. I gave him ten minutes to clear, then I phoned down for some sandwiches and beer, consumed this modest repast and went to bed.

I overslept the next morning, which was bad, since I had

an important engagement. I rose hastily, dressed hastily and applied my disguise hastily. I was still patting my false beard into place as I climbed into the cab Ferdy had procured for me. I gave the address, a street corner in the centre of town, and did some more work on my disguise as we eased through the traffic. I got out of the taxi and looked across the road. Good, he was still at his post, in an unmarked Toyota, looking exactly like a detective constable in an unmarked Toyota.

I crossed the road and then sauntered towards him. Pelham was screening the flow of pedestrians, a massive frown of concentration on his massive face. He screened me and failed to react. Thick dolt! I'd told him I'd be bearded. I crossed the street, circled round and then sauntered towards him again. He looked at his watch and started his engine. I dashed to the Toyota and climbed in beside him. He looked round indignantly.

'Do you mind?' he exclaimed haughtily. 'This is a private vehicle.'

'It's me, Albert, you knuckle-head,' I exclaimed. 'I told you I'd be bearded. Do you want me to walk past again so you can jump me?'

He shook his head glumly.

'One of the lads might see. There's a stake-out across the road. We'd better skip it.'

'As you say. But it's a pretty low-profile arrest when the suspect has to chase the policeman.'

'Any road, I'm bringing you in. I don't suppose there'll be any questions.'

Twenty minutes later, purged of disguise, I sat opposite Superintendent Bowen again. We were in his office.

'Pelham nabbed you?' he asked sceptically.

'Yes. Well – he spotted me. When he beckoned me into his car I wasn't about to make a break for it. That lad's pure muscle. Anyway, I thought it was about time we met again.'

'I've been listening to your broadcasts, Mr Shoestring. They irritate me.'

'I'm sorry about that.'

'They irritate me a great deal. You see, we're checking everything out in a routine way and you're poncing about playing the hero.'

'It's my job, Mr Bowen.'

'I appreciate that. And it's my job to clip your wings.'

'Won't look good – if you lock me up. The fans ——'

'The fans are howling, Mr Shoestring. My switchboard's jammed with your supporters. I wasn't going to lock you up, anyway. What I require is your passport.'

'My passport? No deal, I'm taking the first flight East. You heard my broadcast.'

'Unwise of you, Mr Shoestring. The fact is I can't have my chief suspect soaring out of the country. You've no idea how many people love to criticise the police. I'd stop a lot of flak if I let you go, Mr Shoestring.'

'You know damned well I'm not a murderer.'

'No, I don't. My instinct – which is a pretty trusty instrument – tells me that you're not. But no one's instinct is perfect. The fact is we haven't got any other suspects at present. So you either voluntarily surrender your passport to me or I lock you up. Take your choice.'

'You're putting me out of the running.'

'Oh, don't be childish. There's nothing in the Philippines. The answer is here – probably at Buttercups.'

'How do you figure it, then?'

'I don't mind telling you. But it's got to be off the record. If anything I say in this office goes out over the air you'll be facing a serious charge of obstructing the police.'

'Fair deal.'

'Well, I don't reckon it very far at present. But I have an idea she was mixed up with some of the villainy that was planned at Buttercups.'

'What was that?'

'You wouldn't believe the half of it – gambling, prostitution, drugs – a lot of the big boys stayed at Buttercups from time to time. And I have an idea that some of them met their executioner there.'

'What do you mean?'

'In the last six years, three villains have been hit in different parts of the country. Same style of killing in every case. They'd all stayed at Buttercups shortly before. We've thought for a long tim that there was a connection.'

'You mean, they were fingered there?'

'Something like that.'

'Then find out who was there at the same time as all three of them.'

'What an excellent idea. The only thing is the hit man might not conveniently have used the same name. Then he might not have been a guest but just a visitor.'

'And are you suggesting this hired killer murdered Maria?'

'No. It's possible but unlikely since the three men were all shot. I just think Maria got in the way of something or was mixed up in something that was very unhealthy. I keep an open mind as to whether she was a villain herself.'

'She wasn't.'

'It must be nice to be capable of such certainty, Mr Shoestring. I admit it can pay off if you happen to have made up your mind the right way. But in the long run it's better to keep an open mind and amass evidence.'

'You stick to your methods and I'll live with mine.'

'You've got no choice. But we can always take advice. Now, which is it to be? Incarceration or your passport?'

'Passport.'

'Right, I'll send a panda with you to pick it up.'

'You're nobbling me.'

'We're both shooting at the same target, Mr Shoestring.'

'Have you got any leads? Anything from your forensic people?'

He shook his head grimly.

'No, the lab hasn't come up with anything. Oh, we're satisfied that she didn't die where we found her. And we've fixed the time of death to three hours after you drove her into Bristol. I should add that it's plus or minus two so you're not in the clear. We've not got much else.'

'No one heard a car in that neck of the woods?'

'Unhappily not.'

'Would you like me to put out a request for anyone who did?'

He looked thoughtful.

'I don't see why not. But no reports on the police investigation.'

'I'm not keen on cell life, Superintendent.'

'Then off you go, Mr Shoestring. I'll temporarily look after your passport for you but you can pursue your investigation and make your broadcasts. Let's keep it civilised.'

'Let's do that.'

He rose from his seat and escorted me out of his office. Then he made arrangements for a receipt for my passport to be prepared. When it was ready, he signed it and sent me off with a uniformed constable in a panda. Back at the house, I gave the constable the passport and he gave me the receipt. Then he departed and I went up to Erica's bedroom. I soon uncovered the whisky from her childish hiding place amongst her undies and drank a few shots. Then I went and retrieved my car and drove to the station.

'Any hot tips on tape, sweet mistress?' I asked Sonia hopefully.

'None, valiant warrior for righteousness. Are you still on the run?'

'No. The local fuzz and I have reached a compromise.'

'I'm delighted to hear it.'

'Any chance of a chin-wag with Don?'

'No. He's closeted, believe it or not, with a bishop and an actress.'

'As the receptionist said to the private eye. Well, what shall I do?'

'Go and hunt killers. Clear your name.'

'Not so simple. They've clipped my wings. How long will Don be?'

'Who can say?'

'Are you sure there's nothing on the tape?'

'Loads and loads of sympathy. But no clues.'

'I'll just have a listen.'

I took the three tapes she proffered and went into an empty office and played some of them. It was heart-warming, all right, but it wasn't detection. The people of Avonmouth were solidly behind their favourite eye but none of them could make a plausible suggestion as to who might have strangled Maria Calderes. Any number of implausible suggestions but nothing ——

'You wanted to see me, Eddie?' asked Don, having thrust open the door.

'Just for a minute, Don.'

He consulted his watch.

'That's about my limit. I've got a bishop and an actress coming to see me.'

'I thought you'd just seen a bishop and an actress.'

'I'm seeing loads of them. An amusing new slot I've dreamed up.'

'I don't think I'm ready for it. The police have confiscated my passport.'

Don closed the door behind him and approached. He sat down opposite me.

'Why?'

I shrugged.

'I'm still their only suspect. They don't want to have to extradite me from the Philippines.'

'Were you serious about that?'

'About what?'

'Going to the Philippines.'

'Of course.'

'You'd have had to fund it, you know. The station hasn't got that kind of money.'

I gazed at him in astonishment.

'You'd have begrudged me that? To clear my name? With all the radio mileage I'm getting out of the investigation?'

Don sighed.

'Eddie, anything you can do there, the police can do better. Anyway, it's academic now.'

'No, it's not.'

'How do you mean?'

'I want to send someone as my deputy. Bob or Terry Morgan.'

'Out of the question.'

'Don ——'

'Look, Eddie, let's get this straight. In the circumstances, it's just possible that I could have swung it with the board for you to go. But anyone else – it's just not on.'

'Is that your last word?'

'No, I've got a lot more in reserve. Eddie, do some sleuthing around here – or in London, if you must. No one's going to the Philippines – not on a Radio West expense account anyway. And now, I mustn't keep Bishop Fuller waiting.'

'He'll probably be diverting himself with the actress.'

Don chuckled.

'It's got possibilities, no?'

'No,' I said bitchily. 'Pure corn.'

'Staple of show-biz. Sorry, Eddie.'

And he left briskly. I left, a moment later, less briskly. What now, Shoestring? And, of course, I knew what now. The necessary next step had been forming in my mind the minute Don had started putting the dampers on. It involved smoked salmon, a good Chablis, a poulet au vin blanc, a salad of endives, a selection of cheeses and a bottle of good claret. I spent the rest of the afternoon, first assembling and then preparing the goodies. Everything was well in hand when the front door opened in an agitated sort of way and Erica called: 'Eddie? Are you there?'

I pranced out of the kitchen in my chef's apron to reassure her.

'I'm here, darling.'

'But why? Aren't the police looking for you?'

'Not any more. Superintendent Bowen and I have reached a gentleman's agreement. From now on, we work in co-operation. To celebrate, I've prepared us a sumptuous meal.'

'But shouldn't you be prowling through the underworld?

Won't the trail go cold?'

'No, the police are taking care of the routine stuff. You and I have to plan the creative bit. And what better way to do it than over dinner?'

'Candles?' exclaimed Erica in wonderment. 'You have spared no effort. You want something.'

'Your company and your support.'

'Is that all?'

'Absolutely. Now, I've got to finish the potatoes – rather gimmicky but delicious dish involving saffron and leeks – so if you want to change ——'

'Why should I want to change?'

'No reason. Just thought we might slip out after dinner and dance at the King's or some other classy joint. Make an evening of it.'

'Who's paying?' asksd Erica, a shade aggressively, I felt. 'I am.'

The meal was.superb. The wine was nectar. We became very merry. The merriness persisted as we drove to a nice night-spot in the gorge. It began to fray a little during our third dance.

'What's the matter?' asked Erica.

'The matter? Nothing's the matter. I'm having a tremendous time.'

'Then why did you sigh like that?'

'Like what?'

'Like an Arab who's remembered the oil's running out.'

'I wasn't aware that I had sighed.'

'It was like a sudden gale in the neighbourhood of my ear.'

'Oh, I suppose I was brooding on the investigation. I've come up against a little obstacle.'

'What obstacle?'

'Shall we sit the rest of this one out?'

'Perhaps we'd better. What obstacle have you come up against?'

'The police have got my passport. If I hadn't given it to them, they would have locked me up.'

'Really? Well, it's not surprising in the circumstances. So

what?'

'So it means I can't go to the Philippines.'

'Does that matter?'

'Yes. My instinct tells me that the answer's there.'

'If it is the police will find it.'

'Not necessarily. Anyway, I'm still competing with them. If I break this case, not only do I clear my name but I assure my future. You can see that.'

'I suppose so. So what's to be done?'

'Didn't you say the other day that you've got a little leave coming to you?'

'Yes. I've still got – oh no! I don't believe it. You're not suggesting ——'

'You could go as my deputy. I should think a couple of days, maybe even one, would do the trick. I'd tell you exactly what steps to take.'

'I hate flying.'

'I know. That's why I hesitated before mentioning it.'

'Well, just keep hesitating. I am not going to fly half-way round the world on some – no!'

I sighed again, even more mournfully. Erica said irritably: 'It's no good, Eddie. Just stop that. It's too much to ask.'

'You're right. It is. Okay, I'll take my chances. You know the stakes. You work for the police. You know the pressures on them to get a suspect into court. You know——'

'I know you're an unscrupulous bastard. That's what all the fine nosh and dancing's been about, isn't it? It's just another of your rotten softening-up operations.'

'Yes,' I admitted. 'I was desperate. I couldn't think of anyone to do the job but you. You see, if I'd sent someone from the station, it wouldn't have been the same. You and I have worked together for so long now. You know my methods.'

'But I'm not Doctor Watson. Oh hell, I suppose I'll have to.'

'Erica,' I exclaimed reverently. 'I'm so – well, I'm – thank you, darling. It'll be worth it, you'll see. It'll be a sound investment.'

'I can't let you – hang on. What did you say? Did I hear the word "investment"?'

'It'll pay off a hundred-fold. I'll get a raise. My job will be safe. We'll ——'

'Silence! Eddie, who is financing this expedition?'

'How do you mean?' I asked innocently.

'Money. Cash. For airline tickets and hotels. Who's paying?'

'It won't cost much. I know a fellow in the travel business who ——'

'I didn't ask how much it would cost. I asked: who is putting up the money?'

'You've got a few hundred in the bank, haven't you?'

It was about at this stage that she rose to her feet and stalked haughtily out of the night-club. Nor, when I hurried after her would she exchange a word with me. She did consent to let me drive her home, although she maintained a stony silence the whole way, and when we arrived she just marched up to her bedroom and locked herself in.

Well, to cut a long story short – and because of Erica's basically sweet nature it wasn't nearly as long a story as I'd anticipated – it was about noon the next day that she cracked.

'What the hell do you expect me to find in the Philippines, anyway?'

'If I knew that, there wouldn't be any point in your going. It's just that my instinct tells me that you'll hit something – perhaps trivial in itself – which will put me on the right track.'

'And I'm to fork out a thousand quid in that vague hope?'

'Erica,' I said reproachfully. 'It's not going to cost you a penny. I'll owe it to you.'

'You will?' she asked eagerly. 'If I'd realised that I wouldn't have made such a fuss. Thanks, Eddie.'

She was putting on the heavy sarcasm but we both knew that I'd won. I didn't even bother to sigh deeply again. I just remarked: 'You don't want me locked up, do you?'

D

'No. Shot.'

It was her turn to sigh deeply and she made a meal of it. Then she said: 'All right. Brief me, Shoestring.'

And I did.

Chapter 6

The next day, I drove Erica to Heathrow. Don had used a little Radio West muscle to get us an early flight. Erica and I were thoroughly reconciled by now. Indeed, she seemed excited by the whole adventure. I said goodbye to her at the barrier and then went up to the observation deck and watched her Jumbo jet first ease and then charge down the runway and then head steeply up into the sky as if on an invisible ramp. I watched it bank slightly and then, still climbing, disappear, presumably, towards the Philippines. By the time I got back to Bristol she'd be in India or thereabouts. Amazing.

Then I set off back to Bristol. I drove at a leisurely pace and stopped for a good pub lunch. I intended to spend the week or so until Erica returned pursuing various hopeful lines of inquiry. I didn't expect anything dramatic to happen. But I was wrong. The next day, something did.

The previous afternoon, I'd put out my request, as I'd promised Superintendent Bowen I would, for anyone who'd seen a vehicle in the vicinity of the place where Maria Calderes was found, to phone in. When I got to the station the next morning someone had done. Sonia was quite excited:

'Could be the vital lead, yes?' she asked eagerly.

'Could be,' I agreed.

I phoned Superintendent Bowen and he courteously picked me up and we drove together to visit Mr Daly Mackay, the representative of a Scottish whisky distilling firm who was staying at the Avon Gorge Hotel on a three-day visit to Bristol for the purpose of selling as much whisky as he could. Mr Mackay was clearly in that state of anxiety often found in witnesses who want to be good citizens but can only do so by admitting to misconduct themselves. Mr Mackay insisted to us that he was a very happily married man with three 'bonny kids' who could hardly imagine why he had been, on the night in question, enlaced in a haystack with a Bristol girl he'd met only that night in a disco. I eyed Mr Mackay. He was actually thirty-five but looked much younger. Presumably he had a way of looking in at local discos when on his whisky run. Superintendent Bowen very efficiently put him at his ease. He wasn't concerned with Mr Mackay's moral stature but with any useful information he could give us.

It wasn't much. It seemed that Mr Mackay and Molly, the young disco-dancer in question, had driven out of Bristol intent on finding a quiet spot. None of the spots they'd found had appealed to them as sufficiently quiet until they came to the little lane, connecting two larger roads, near which Maria Calderes' body had been found. About a mile from that spot, Mr Mackay and Molly had appreciatively spotted an open gate leading into a field and, just inside the gate, an attractive-looking haystack. Mr Mackay had promptly turned his Granada off the road and the two had climbed out of it and into the haystack. About half an hour later, a vehicle came along the lane. This was the only one to do so and, vaguely apprehensive lest it might prove to be a farmer concerned about the abuse to his haystack, Mr Mackay had glanced over his shoulder to watch. The vehicle, with dipped headlights he thought, had passed at about thirty or thirty-five miles an hour. Because of the relative positions of the gate and himself, Mr Mackay hadn't seen much but he had thought that the vehicle might have been a Bedford van. Naturally, it occurred to both Inspector Bowen and I to ask: what of Molly? What had she seen? Mr Mackay had no idea what Molly might or might not have seen because he hadn't been particularly concerned with conversation at the time and she hadn't offered any comment. He did agree that, because of their relative positions at the crucial moment, Molly would have been in a position to see rather more than he did but he hadn't seen Molly since and so hadn't been able to inquire. Nor did he know where he could locate her. They had met that night, passed an hour or two in a haystack and then parted for ever – or so he had thought. He had no address for her. She was just a girl called Molly who danced, or had on at least one occasion danced, in the I Ching Discotheque.

'We'll soon find her,' said Superintendent Bowen cheerfully. 'Thank you very much, Mr Mackay.'

'You won't – that is, you're not going to ——' asked Mr Mackay anxiously.

'We're not,' Superintendent Bowen assured him. 'We must have your address, of course. But there's unlikely to be any further involvement. Thank you again.'

And we departed.

This, of course, was police country. It might have taken me a week to find Molly or I might never have found her. But they would, I felt convinced.

At about three in the afternoon, I had a call from the Super. They had located her. He invited me to join him in a chat with the young lady who, it seemed, worked in a small plastics factory.

I was just leaving the station when Sonia came pattering after me.

'Call for you, Eddie.'

'Get it on the tape, would you, fragrant Goddess? I've got an important date.'

'I think you'd better take this one.'

Sonia knew the score. She wouldn't have pressed me if her instinct hadn't told her it could be important. I glanced at my watch. I returned to her desk and took the call.

'Hello? Eddie Shoestring here,' I said.

'It's me,' said a voice in which hysteria palpably quavered. I knew the voice, even through the hysteria. The last time I had heard it, it had been boasting about its literary grandfather. The Mantis. 'I'm in danger. Help me. I need your help.'

'All right,' I said soothingly. 'Calm down. What kind of

danger?'

'Every kind. Death. They wouldn't stop at that. They haven't stopped at that. That's what I wrote. That's why they stole it. But it won't stop there. Because I can write it again. That's why they'll try to kill me. You've got to come here. You've got to protect me.'

'Please, Mr – er – Carew something, isn't it?'

'What does my name matter? It's Carew-Prendergast. Will you come and get me – now!'

'Where are you?'

'I'm in Bath, of course. I'm in a phone booth near the bus station. As soon as I found it was missing, I ran straight out. I understood. I've probably been followed. I'm in terrible danger. Come at once.'

'Calm down. What was missing?'

'My manuscript, of course. They've stolen it.'

'Who's stolen it?'

'Cranston. No, not Cranston. He wouldn't do it himself. He wouldn't get his hands dirty. The big boys never do. They hire people to do their dirty work. But he's behind it. If I'm killed, just remember that. Cranston's behind it. Promise ——'

'Shut up! Look, I'm willing to help you. But I must know exactly what's happened. Tell me in ——'

And just then the pips started pipping. I waited, feeling a slight tinge of real anxiety for the Mantis. Then there was the slight electronic gasp of the line being opened again.

'Hello? Hello? Hello?' cried the Mantis desperately.

'It's okay. I'm still here. Now tell me exactly what's happened.'

'I finished my shift and went up to my room. I went to get my manuscript and it wasn't there. I keep it under the mattress and it wasn't there.'

'Had the room been broken into?'

'How should I know? Let's see. I used my key. It seemed to be normal.'

'Was anything else missing?'

'Don't be silly! Of course nothing else was missing. It

was my manuscript they were after. And now they're after me. Come at once, Shoestring. At once!'

'Look, there's no question of my coming at once. I've got an important interview with a witness. I can't afford to miss it. Now, this is what I suggest. I think you're grossly exaggerating but if you're really worried, go to the police and tell them ——'

'They won't ——'

'Just listen to me, Carew-Prendergast!' I exhorted, feeling an impulse to laugh at the pompous name. 'If you don't want to go to the police, come and see me. I can give you some time in about an hour. Come to the radio station and I'll meet you there.'

'Meet me at the bus terminus.'

I sighed.

'All right, I'll meet you at the bus terminus. But I can't be absolutely certain when I'll get there. I'll be as quick as I can.'

'I'll wait for you. I won't move. I'll wait for you at the bus terminus. You promise? You promise you'll come?'

'I promise.'

'Don't let me down, Shoestring.'

'I'll see you at the bus station.'

With which I hung up. Could there be anything in his very real alarm? There could be but it seemed to me far more likely that he'd misplaced his manuscript or someone had made his bed and confiscated it by mistake or – some trivial explanation. Anyway, nothing much could happen to him in the next hour in public places. And I didn't want to miss what Molly had to say. That might help nail a real murderer and clear my name.

'Was I right to get you back?' asked Sonia anxiously.

'You were, astute one,' I assured her. 'And now I'm late. Must dash.'

And I hurried out to my car and drove down to the factory where Superintendent Bowen and a lean detective-sergeant were questioning Molly. She proved to be a delightful young lady, highly intelligent and completely

103

unabashed at the situation.

'It's a good place to go,' she explained. 'I often use it.'

'You mean, you led him there?' asked Bowen.

'No. Men don't like to be led. They like to think that they're leading. And they hate to think you've used the place before. But I sort of nudged him there, if you see what I mean.'

'Why is it a good place?' asked Bowen.

'Quiet and comfortable – two main things. No traffic.'

'But on this night there was some traffic.'

'That night there was a dark blue or black short-wheel-base Bedford van going East.'

Bowen and the sergeant exchanged a look.

'That's a very exact description,' said Bowen.

'I know. I had plenty of time to observe it. I was on my back.'

Bowen actually made a harrumph in his throat as police officers do on the screen when they are faintly embarrassed.

'Do you know a lot about motor vehicles?' he asked.

'I know all about them. My dad runs a garage. I've helped him in it since I was a kiddy. I wanted to be a racing driver first. But then I figured it wouldn't be too sexy. It's sexy for a man but I don't think it would be for a girl. So now I want to be a model. I wouldn't object to nude modelling.'

'No, well – can you tell us anything more about this van?'

'Not much. It was doing about thirty and it was on dipped lights, which was a bit funny. Was the murderer in it?'

'What murderer?'

'Oh, come on. I listen to Shoestring. It's about that Japanese girl that got done, isn't it?'

'Doesn't it make you think?' asked Bowen unexpectedly.

'How do you mean?' asked Molly.

'That girl was murdered within a mile of where you were with a strange man. Doesn't it make you think?'

Molly shrugged.

'Not really. I wouldn't go with any weirdo – just straight sex.'

'Can you always be sure?'

'I suppose not. But it's either take a chance or give up sex. No contest, is there?'

Bowen sighed and said to her: 'Well, the sergeant will take your name and address. We may need to call on you again. And if I were you ——'

'Oh, don't give me good advice. It takes all the fun out of life.'

The good superintendent shook his head sadly and, beckoning me, strolled away. We went out of the empty staff canteen, where we'd been interviewing the girl, and took a turn in the cluttered yard. We agreed that she'd been a remarkably good witness. We'd got something to go on. Bowen said they'd start checking out all the dark blue or black Bedford vans in the country but obviously it was going to be one hell of a big job. And I left soon because I wanted to get to the bus station and meet the Mantis.

It was the rush hour. The car fumed and I fumed and it took me a half hour to crawl the mile or so to the bus station. I was still edging towards it in a line of cars when I first spied the Mantis. He was standing at the window inside the waiting room, peering out nervously. I waved but he didn't see me. I edged closer and then, frustrated by the clogged vehicles, pulled up on a double-yellow and bumped the car up on to the pavement. I got out and waved furiously across the two bus lanes until he saw me. He seemed to stiffen and then his face vanished from the window and a moment later, he emerged from the door of the waiting room and started trotting across the bus lanes towards me. And then it happened.

An orange Mini-Clubman shot out from the niche just outside the bus waiting area and bore down on the Mantis. I know the details because the police pieced it together afterwards but at the time I just saw a streak of orange and heard an engine roaring. The Mini must have been doing something near forty when it hit the Mantis. And that's when things started to go wrong. Not for the Mantis, who'd already had his share of misfortune for the day, but for his would-be assassin. The Mini hit the Mantis square and it proved to be too square. Instead of being hurled against a bus or disappearing under the Mini, the Mantis shot straight up in the air, a vision that might have been a comic one of flailing limbs and rotating body if it hadn't had a grim side, and came down on the bonnet of the Mini. There it remained, almost completely blocking the driver's vision. There was a scream of brakes. The Mini decelerated sharply and the body – as it seemed – stayed put. Then – and I was already running towards the scene – I saw the dark figure of the driver craning this way and that to see where he was going. He picked up speed slightly and the Mini swung madly from side to side. He was trying to dislodge the obstruction. But the Mantis was hooked by his clothing – again as the police subsequently discovered – on both windscreen wipers and, although he jerked horribly about on the bonnet, he remained in place. Then the door of the Mini opened somewhat and a man's head poked out. I saw that the driver was wearing a cloth cap with a low peak, but that was all I could see. The Mini headed for a gap between buses, once more accelerating. But the gap was a narrow one and, to prevent possible decapitation, the driver had to pull in his head immediately, causing the Mini to veer from side to side again. It hit the first bus at a glancing angle, was deflected off it on to the other bus, which it struck at a sharper angle with a dull crump and finally wobbled through the gap, the Mantis still secured on the bonnet. I was shouting by then: 'Get him! Get him!' as I belted on foot after the rogue Mini.

After having cleared the bus area, the door of the Mini opened slightly again and the head protruded. The vehicle charged across a crowded isthmus of pedestrians, scattering a queue but fortunately not hitting anyone, and finally disappeared up a narrow one-way street, near the bus terminal, the Mantis still lodged on its bonnet. Because of my angle of approach, I was not, although on foot, far behind it. I reached the street corner and, beginning to feel pretty puffed, turned up it. The Mini had stopped some ten yards into the street. A man was standing beside it, tugging fiercely at the limp figure on the bonnet. I tried to run towards him but the best I could manage was a rapid stagger. He heard my faltering footsteps and turned towards me. And I caught a glimpse of the lower part of his face. I concentrated on that. The clothing he wore, which included gloves, would, I knew, disappear for ever. But he couldn't tie a stone to his face and drop it over a canal bridge. However, the peak of his cloth cap, doubtless selected for the purpose, concealed most of his face and a mist of exhaustion was beginning to cloud my vision. I tried to speed up and saw, at last, the figure of the Mantis slide from the bonnet. Then, with a strength and savagery equally remarkable, the driver hurled the broken Mantis to one side, jumped back into the driving seat and engaged gear. I was almost on him by then and, from behind, I heard the rapid pad of fresher footsteps. I touched the Mini – and it slipped ahead up the one-way street, gathering speed.

I leaned against a wall and pulled out a scrap of paper and a pen. It seemed superfluous since that Mini, buckled and bashed and probably drenched in blood, must be about the most conspicuous car in Bristol now, but I wrote down its licence number. Then I concentrated on feeding oxygen to my red blood cells. While I gasped, I watched several people clustered round the remnants, as it seemed to me they must be, of the Mantis. And the first twinges of guilt began to prick me. He'd been right. He had been marked down for the chop. And I'd let him down. Not too much guilt, Shoestring, you behaved sensibly, I told myself. You had no way of knowing how serious it was. But if you fail, you fail. And the mangled thing lying just ahead of me on the pavement was proof that I'd failed. He must have known a whole lot more than I'd dreamed he had. His manuscript must have been dynamite. There are all kinds of legal ways of gagging people. And if those fail, you tend, if you're a hood of some kind, to scare them a little. But that orange Mini and its visored driver hadn't been just for frighteners. It had been for real.

What had happened? Someone had stolen the Mantis's manuscript and somehow missed catching up with him. Then the hit man had cruised about Bath and found him. But the Mantis, obeying my instructions, had stayed in nice public view. He'd taken the bus to Bristol and waited for me in the waiting room, safe and secure amongst people. And then I'd arrived and waved cordially – luring him to destruction. Because, when the watcher had seen me and seen the Mantis start towards me, he'd realised that time was getting very short. Maybe he knew who I was and maybe he just thought I might be fuzz but he'd decided there wasn't a moment to lose. And he'd made his spectacular play.

Well, he wouldn't get far. He must have blood on him from the Mantis. He was driving a car that might just as well have MURDERER written on it in big red letters. About half of Bristol had seen the attempt. And here was a police car hee-hawing up now to spread the message and start the beaters closing in on him. Which is why it was almost incredible that, three hours later, I was saying to Superintendent Bowen:

'How? I just don't understand how.'

The Superintendent shrugged slightly.

'He just got out of the car and walked away.'

'And no one saw him? No one?'

'No one that we've yet found. Hit-and-run drivers are always the devil to catch.'

'Yes, if they clip a cyclist in a country lane at two a.m. I wouldn't have thought the same applied to a murderer who played snooker with half the cars in Bristol at rush hour.'

'He's not a murderer.'

'Not for want of trying.'

'That's your opinion, Mr Shoestring.'

'It's not. I've told you all about it.'

'But have you told us the truth? We have no knowledge of this mysterious manuscript. As far as we know, a hotel barman was knocked down by what may have been a drunk.'

'Okay. How bad is the Mantis – the barman?'

'Pretty bad. Fractured skull and likewise both legs and three ribs. And he's lost a lot of blood. One thing's certain, he won't be able to confirm your story for a week or ten.'

'What about witnesses?'

'Hundreds. I believe the French call it an embarrassment of witnesses. If you have too many they all tell different stories.'

'No pattern emerging?'

'Not yet.'

'Evidence?'

'Tons of it. The car to begin with. But, of course, it was stolen. Then there's all kinds of odd items in it, including a cloth cap, a pair of gloves and other articles of clothing. Lots of evidence but no fingerprints.'

'Because of the gloves?'

'Very likely.'

'But ——'

'Yes?'

I shook my head sadly.

'Look, would you be surprised if a man walked into a police station, shot the desk sergeant, walked out again and was never caught?'

'No. Nothing would surprise me. I've come across too many bizarre things in my time. The New York police force once spent ten years trying to catch a counterfeiter who passed dollar bills with George Washington's name misspelled on them. In the end they only caught him by chance because of a fire. He turned out to be a street pedlar. Sometimes you get the breaks and sometimes you don't. But we work on, Mr Shoestring, in our methodical way which often *does* produce results. And since you seem to be our chief witness to this business, perhaps you'd now concentrate on those mug-shots.'

I'd been turning through the pages of the villains' album while we'd been talking. But he was right, I hadn't really been concentrating. I went back to the start and went slowly and patiently through the book.

'Well?' asked the Superintendent.

'I don't know. I don't think so. I only had a glimpse, from the nose down.'

'His chin. Concentrate on his chin. What was his chin like?'

I thought hard. Had there been anything even remotely remarkable about the murderer's chin?

'He had a moustache,' I said suddenly. 'That's funny. I was concentrating on his chin and I suddenly saw his moustache.'

'Well, now try zooming in on the moustache and perhaps you'll get the chin.'

I closed my eyes. After a moment or two, I opened them again and shook my head.

'An ordinary chin – nothing special.'

'Well, you'd forgotten the moustache. What kind was it?'

'Sandy. Thin. Kind of upper-class moustache.'

'That gives us something. He had sandy hair and style. Go through the book again. Concentrate on the moustaches.'

I went through the book again and finally came up with a possible. The Superintendent took a quick glance at it and shook his head.

'How can you be sure?' I asked.

'That's Billy Smart. He's a midget – well, only about five five. Your chap was tall, wasn't he?'

'Yes, around six foot, I'd say.'

'All right,' said the Superintendent, shutting the book. 'You can go. Hang on, you might as well have a look at the outsiders.'

'Who are they?'

'Just three or four that the computer picked out. They're all clean as far as we know – nothing on any of them –but their stays at Buttercups and such details as we've got make them possible candidates.'

He took the heavy book and left his office, returning in a minute or two with an envelope. He pulled out a few photographs and handed them to me. Just then, his door opened

110

behind me and someone said:

'Excuse me, sir, they've brought in Dawkins.'

'Good,' said the Superintendent cheerfully. Then to me: 'I must have a quick word with this one. Be back in a minute.'

I looked through the photographs. There were four of them. None had moustaches but then moustaches can come and go. None of them, however, rang a bell. I stood up, tossing the pictures down on the desk in front of me. I went to the window and gazed out at a policewoman kissing a policeman in a panda car. It was nice to know there was so much *esprit-de-corps* in the local force. I left the window and went back to the desk. The door opened and the Superintendent returned. As he did so, I reached quickly down and turned the pictures face up again. Just as he had entered, I had seen the name on the back of one of them. It was Christopher Dixon. *Chris!*

'Any joy?' asked Superintendent Bowen.

'Not really. A chin's a chin.'

The Inspector went over to his glass-fronted bookcase, which seemed to be packed with fascinating volumes about the law and how to apply it. But he didn't open it. Instead, he took from its top a small silver cup. He said:

'This one was for The Ghost.'

'A fish?' I asked without animation.

'A big pike. It lived in a pond in Northamptonshire with about a hundred other pike. I decided to catch it. I caught six or seven other pike and put them back. I knew they weren't The Ghost.'

'It had a razor slash on its left cheek?'

'I recognised it. I knew its appearance. And in the end I caught it. There was a woman called Marcelle Winters – well, there still is. We put Marcelle on an identity parade and she failed to pick the right, or you might say the wrong, man.'

'Must happen all the time.'

'It does. But it was interesting about Marcelle. She'd been taken hostage after a bank robbery. We nabbed two of the three robbers but the third got away with Marcelle and held her for three weeks. Naturally, he wore a mask but there were dozens of times during those three weeks when she caught a glimpse of him. She escaped on her own – pretty good effort really – and we picked up the villain a few weeks later. And Marcelle couldn't even pick him out of an identity parade. We nailed him because of other evidence but it makes you think.'

'It does.'

'I don't trust IDs. People see visions of what they want to see.'

'Do you think there's a connection between the Mant—— between this incident and Maria Calderes?'

'Possibly. What's "the Mant", Mr Shoestring?'

'Oh – it's a bit shaming now but I thought of him as a praying mantis. He looks a bit like one.'

'Hard, isn't it, to preserve a sense of the humanity of human beings?'

'It is in our game. Will there be anything else, Super-intendent?'

'Not for the present, Mr Shoestring.'

I moved towards the door. The Superintendent coughed.

'Just – well, off the record, Mr Shoestring, I have no doubt as to your innocence. And I think we're in your debt to some extent. I doubt if we'd have got a lead on that Bedford van without you. But officially you're still our only suspect. Try and play it by the book.'

'Word and letter, Superintendent.'

But I had no intention of doing so. As I left, my thoughts were running strongly on Detective Constable Pelham. I hastened down to the Blackmore Tavern but Albert had consumed his hogshead of Guinness and left for the night. Where do detective constables go in the evening? Was it conceivable that Albert had a wife and some little Pelhams? If so, where did they all roost? I tried to picture a family gathering of the Pelhams and saw a grotesque parade of tiny detectives all wearing off-the-peg suits and packed into what was obviously an unmarked police car. Had Albert ever mentioned a family? I racked my brains. The essential trouble was that he'd never mentioned anything. Not a great conversationalist was Albert. But surely he'd have mentioned a wife if there was one. No, Pelham wasn't married. He must live in a bedsitter with a frayed carpet and a gas-ring. Below him was Mrs Landlady who cooked his meals and, for a trifling consideration, took his off-the-peg suits to the dry-cleaners. And, while he favoured the Blackmore Tavern for early evening drinks there must be a pub somewhere in Bristol where Albert spent the bulk of his evening throwing a deadly dart and engulfing enough of the Irish brew to float a corpse. But where was it?

Where? Where? Well, it wouldn't be in any of the grand suburbs and it wouldn't be in the slums. And it wouldn't be where the neat and airy semi-detacheds basked under a single cherry tree or lilac. It would be in an urban area, bleak but respectable, handy for the police station and with a pub or two within plodding range. That narrowed it down a bit. There couldn't be more than a couple of hundred pubs in districts like that.

I couldn't have covered them all. It just seemed like it. I tottered, shortly after eleven, out of The Blenkinsop trying to infer the time from my watch which was showing a definite tendency, although anchored to my wrist, to swoop about like one of those aerobatic kites. I gave up on the time and, reaching my car, attempted to insert the key into the lock. While I was doing so, I brooded resentfully on the name of the pub. 'The Blenkinsop'? What kind of name was that for a pub? Who was Blenkinsop? What was he? That all the boozers commended him? Except Albert. Albert hadn't liked The Blenkinsop. True, he hadn't seemed to favour The Four Feathers, The George, The Grouse and Gin, The Mandarin, The Eel and Cobbler or any of the other ten thousand pubs I had called at during the last ten centuries. Ten centuries? Had I really been pub-crawling that long? Must be some kind of record. Phone the *Guinness Book of Records* – where *was* bloody Albert?

I got the tricky key inserted into the car door and

embarked on the delicate business of unlocking same. It only took about four minutes and then I drove home.

I entered the house trying to recall if I'd knocked down a traffic light on the way. Absurd. Only drunken drivers knock down traffic lights. Must have been the wind. What's that? Phone ringing. Need a drink to face it. Where's Erica's whisky? Is that it? No, that's a souvenir from St Peter's Port. Wouldn't mind a drop of St Peter's port. Or his whisky. Or his – here it is, whisky. Pour myself large measure. Damn. Should have used a glass. Into kitchen for glass. Got glass. Pour large whisky. What's that noise? Gale warning? No, it's phone. Phone ringing somewhere. Stagger to answer phone. Locate it by pure instinct. Answer phone:

'Hello? Erica? Is that you?'

'Eddie? Eddie? Are you all right?'

'Topping, thank you.'

'Are you drunk?'

'Yes, thank you.'

'Oh, Eddie! Can you understand me?'

'Of course. No problem. Certainly. Indeed.'

'Eddie! For God's sake! This is costing money.'

'It is? What is? Oh, the phone call. I don't want you to worry about that, Erica. I want to assure you ——'

'Damn you, will you buck up!'

'Sorry. Been out on a case. Pursuing important contact. Bucked up now. Give it to me straight.'

'Give what to you straight?'

'What? What case are you on? Are we on the same case? Just refresh my memory. Where are you talking from?'

'You bloody pig.'

And she hung up on me.

Chapter 7

I opened my eyes and saw some thick ankles clad in thick, wrinkled stockings. I promptly closed my eyes again. I thought it over. Where was I? At home. Was that right? Yes, I'd made it home. But I should be alone in the house. What were these ankles doing here? Erica? No, no, no. Erica was – yes, she'd gone to the Philippines to do a spot of investigating. I opened my eyes again. No ankles. Should I try to rise? Did I have a headache? I blinked several times rapidly and a faint pealing started in my head. I *did* have a headache but how bad was it? The ankles passed slowly across my field of vision. Erica's ankles? No, no, Erica had nice slim ankles and these were heavy-duty ankles which had undergone a good deal of wear and tear. Besides Erica's ankles were in the Philippines. Did I have a headache? I raised myself slightly and heard two loud screams. The first I recognised as one of my own but the second was a strange scream. It was followed by a voice saying:

'Oh! Oh, Mr Shoestring, you startled me. I didn't know you were awake.'

I had relaxed back into my original position. Softly and carefully, I said: 'Oh, yes. Wide awake. Is that you, Mrs Sweet?'

'That's right, Mr Shoestring. Just come in to tidy up the way Miss Erica wanted.'

'Good, good. She neglected to mention to me you'd be calling. How did you get in, by the way?'

'How do you mean, Mr Shoestring?'

'Did she leave you a key?'

'Oh no, she said you'd let me in. But when I got here, I found the front door wide open. Taking a bit of a risk, isn't it, Mr Shoestring? With all the break-ins we've had round here recently?'

'Yes, I – trifle negligent – er – what time is it, Mrs Sweet?'

'It's half-past twelve.'

'Really? I – erm – had rather an exhausting day yesterday – detecting and so forth.'

'I tried to move you – on to the sofa but you was too heavy. Aren't you going to get up off the floor now, Mr Shoestring?'

'Get up? Oh yes, certainly. Very shortly. Erm, I don't suppose I could trouble you to whip me up a drop of black coffee, could I, Mrs Sweet?'

'The kettle's on. Shall I help you up, Mr ——'

'AAargh! No, just leave me for a moment, Mrs Sweet. You run along into the kitchen and get the coffee and I'll – I'll be up in a – jiffy – or two.'

By the time Mrs Sweet returned with the fragrant infusion I had hoisted myself gingerly on to the sofa and was bringing the world into something approaching soft focus.

'Thank you, Mrs Sweet,' I said pleasantly. 'Just put it there on the side table.'

She did so, remarking: 'Miss Erica rang twice. I tried to wake you but you was out to the world. She was phoning from Manila, wherever that is.'

'It's out there in the – erm – the Pacific, Mrs Sweet. What did Miss Erica want?'

'She was cross, Mr Shoestring, there's no denying it. She said you was to go to hell and that she was coming home tomorrow.'

'Did you tell her that I was – erm – in the room?'

'I had no choice, did I, Mr Shoestring?'

'No, of course not. Did Miss Erica say anything else?'

'She said she'd do what you asked her. She said she hated it there – in the Pacific, you say? And she was booked on a flight home tomorrow. And there was no good phoning her any more because she was fed up with you and wouldn't answer the phone.'

'I see. As you may have gathered, Mrs Sweet, I'm not quite myself this morning. There's a technique I often use in these circumstances. It involves immersing my head in cold water and then walking round the block. Several of these cycles usually effect a marvellous improvement. I wonder if you could fill the kitchen sink with cold water for me, Mrs Sweet, and then give me a hand to get in there?'

'Hangover, is it?' asked Mrs Sweet glumly, but she went off into the kitchen and I heard the sink being filled.

Five dunks and circuits of the block and I felt somewhat restored. I contemplated trying to trace Erica in Manila but I didn't know her hotel and it might take hours. Meanwhile there was a trail getting cold. I set off for the police station to try and make discreet contact with DC Pelham and I struck lucky.

Half-way there, while fretting at a traffic light, I noticed a conspicuous street cleaner trailing an electric rubbish float. I gazed at him in stupefaction. Could Pelham really suppose that he looked like anything but a detective constable pulling an electric rubbish float? I wound down the car window and called:

'Albert? Albert, over here. It's me, Eddie.'

Albert's head jerked up and he glanced nervously from side to side. One of his great hands lifted and he waved me silent with all the inconspicuousness of a karate expert chopping bricks in half. I sighed. The traffic lights changed and I swung quickly ahead of a honking and enraged driver into a side street, parked my car where it shouldn't have been parked and belted back after Albert. I walked past him at a brisk pace, saying clearly out of the corner of my mouth:

'Take the next right, Albert. I must have a word with you.'

Then I continued on to the corner, turned right myself and stationed myself a few yards up the street noting, with approval, that there was a pub called The Three Feathers only a little further up the street. I waited and before long Albert shuffled round the corner trailing his rubbish float.

'You shouldn't do that, Eddie,' he said reproachfully, when he reached me.

'Sorry, Albert, but it's urgent. I spent all last evening looking for you. Where do you drink in the evening, anyway?'

'I went to the pictures with my wife.'

'You've got a wife?' I said, trying to keep the incredulity from my voice.

'Well, she's not really my wife.'

'Ah – yes.' I waited a moment for Albert to elaborate on his unconventional domestic arrangements but he remained dumb and I resumed, 'The thing is, Albert, I need some information and you're the only one that can help me. Oh, that's a spot of luck. There seems to be a pub just up there. I'll tell you about it over a Guinness.'

'I'm watching out for Car Johnny.'

'Really? Well, he might be in the boozer, mightn't he?'

'Don't think I'd better, Eddie.'

But his eyes lingered on the welcoming sign.

'Must be thirsty work tugging that great thing around.'

'It's electric.'

'Still – lot of hoofing. A pint'd freshen you up.'

'Just one then.'

'All I've got time for, Albert.'

We ambled at his float's top speed up to the pub, abandoned the graceless machine and went into the public where I ordered a pint of Guinness for Albert and a large scotch for myself. While we consumed them, I told Albert what I needed. I needed all the particulars he could get me on a computer suspect called Christopher Dixon. Albert listened impassively. Then he shook his head ponderously.

'I can't do that, Eddie. More than my job's worth.'

'Listen, Albert, no one will ever know. I just want to check this one out. No sweat, no hassle, no strong-arm. It's just an elimination ploy. If I should strike lucky, I'd share the credit with you. You wouldn't object to being a sergeant, would you?'

'It's against regulations.'

For a moment I thought he meant that an instruction had been issued that DC Pelham must not be promoted but then I realised that what he really meant was that doing what I asked was against regulations.

'Albert,' I urged persuasively, 'you don't think Montgomery got to command the Eighth Army by following regulations, do you?'

'Never thought about it.'

'No leader of men has ever lived by regulations, Albert. Have you ever asked yourself why you're still a DC and lesser men are inspectors and superintendents?'

'Some have got more intelligence than me.'

'That may have a bearing on the matter. But there's also boldness and daring to be considered, isn't there? Ten cases of Guinness.'

Albert brooded for a while and then said:

'Ten?'

'Ten, Albert. Now just write your address down here for me, so I can get the Guinness delivered.'

He took my proffered ball-point and wrote his address in a surprisingly neat and delicate hand.

'Now when can you get it for me, Albert?'

'Have to wait for a good opportunity, Eddie. Tomorrow or next day.'

'I want it this afternoon, Albert.'

'You must be ——'

'Ten cases, Albert.'

'Well, you keep an eye on my rubbish float. I'll slip back to HQ and see if there's any chance.'

'Done, Albert.'

He drained his Guinness and I my scotch and soda and we left to find that the rubbish float had gone. Albert gave a hoarse cry. I grabbed him by the arm and pulled him after me towards my car. When we reached it, a traffic warden was just affixing a ticket to it. Like all traffic wardens she did this with maddening deliberation. Two minutes later, Albert and I roared off and twelve minutes later we found a schoolgirl pulling the rubbish float up a shopping

119

street while five of her depraved classmates screamed and gambolled inside it. Passers-by eyed the jamboree with disapproval. Albert decided not to arrest them since the necessary explanations back at the station would be embarrassing. He resumed possession of his machine, after sternly warning the rude little girls about the hazards and penalties of joy-riding, and, when we were safely out of sight, handed the horrid cart over to me. He showed me a picture of Car Johnny and told me to keep my eye out for him and for the next hour I trundled the float up and down Hill Street looking for Car Johnny. Then Albert returned and I put my tie back on. An hour later I was on the London train, reading the photostat Albert had given me.

Christopher Dixon, it seemed, was an art dealer. He came from a good family. His father was Sir Roderick Dixon, QC. Christopher was thirty-five years old and a bachelor but one with an enthusiasm for the opposite sex. He was often observed in the company of beautiful and, usually, well-born ladies. As far as was known, his business was successful. He had no criminal record. The only reason why his name and photograph were known to the police was that the computer had spotted the fact that he had twice stayed at Buttercups a month or two before a notorious villain had been assassinated in another part of the country. Since the ratio of respectable to criminal at Buttercups was about ten to one, the odds against Mr Dixon being a crook, never mind a murderer, were very high. But his name *was* Chris. Could he be the father of Maria Calderes' apparently non-existent child? It was unlikely. Chris was, after all, a common name. I brooded in the train. And again something I'd forgotten – something relevant – nagged at me. It was something Maria had said to me on that last ride into Bristol, the last time anyone, as far as the police knew, had seen her alive. I replayed the drive in my memory, forcing myself to go through it moment by moment from beginning to end. Once I paused, feeling a tremor of excitement. It was there – almost. The key phrase – or had I already repeated it to myself? Was it just that I couldn't quite see – although a part of my mind knew – *why* it was a key phrase? It was no good. I couldn't recapture it by, as it were, mental brute force. I sighed and turned to the newspaper.

It was half-past five when I reached Paddington. It was unlikely that I would get to Bond Street before the shops shut but I found a taxi and went there nonetheless. I wanted to get a look at Mr Dixon's establishment. It was not actually in Bond Street but in Mitre Passage which runs off it and connects with Albemarle Street. It had a substantial frontage and it was closed. I stood in front of its windows, inspecting the contents. Framed and featured, on a gilt easel, was a large, florid painting that looked a bit like the child of an unnatural marriage between Rubens and Constable. The landscape was chaste but the three nymphs sporting in a glade were plump, fleshy specimens. It was by a painter called Bagehot, whom I'd never heard of, but then I was never strong on fine art. There was also a nice bronze of a ballet dancer in the window and a few sporting prints. I peered through the glass. In the main showroom were canvases ranged all round the walls and three or four more bronzes, including one of an Indian boy – at least he wore a turban – walking a cheetah. Very nice but nothing that I'd particularly want to wake up to. I stepped back and looked at the elegant, gilt-lettered sign above the door. It said Dixon & Purdue, Fine Art.

There was nothing more to do that evening except find a hotel. The words Ritz and Claridges flamed in my mind but I sternly dismissed them. No point antagonising Don. No, I'd stay at some decent place nearby. I walked down Lorenzo Street looking for a hotel. Passed one or two but they seemed very unpretentious indeed. Then, on the corner of Miramar Street, I saw just the inn. It had an awning under which stood a liveried doorman but it was a small, human, comfortable-looking place. I went in, noting with approval that the hall, with its white and gilt columns and olive-green carpeting, was discreetly elegant and I inquired at the desk for a room. They had one and showed it to me. It was most acceptable and I took it on the spot. It wasn't until I studied the menu that evening that I began to have misgivings. The place was pricey all right and the food turned out to be superb. After dinner, I had three whiskies in the bar and struck up a conversation with a horse-breeder who told me that he'd just bought a 'nice little filly' for only 'fifty thou'. My misgivings increased. Breakfast in the morning was positively poetic and my total bill, which they handed to me at the desk, was stunning. It was about, as far as I could judge, fifty per cent more than the Ritz or Claridges would have charged. I had stumbled, with the unerring instinct of a poor man who appreciates the finer things of life, on one of the most prestigious hotels in London, as I explained to Don later.

Still dazed from the blow, I ambled out into Grosvenor Square and walked about in it for ten minutes or so collecting my thoughts. I didn't want to get to Dixon & Purdue, Fine Art, too early. I had an idea that in any case art dealers didn't open very early. I mean duchesses don't bustle out to buy a Vermeer the way the average housewife nips down to the supermarket, do they?

I had a leisurely coffee in the best place I could find. When I got the bill for it, I realised that London had developed a great talent for mopping up any spare currency that might, as the politicians put it, be slopping about in the economy. My economy was by now thoroughly mopped-up. Still, what the hell? I headed for Dixon & Purdue.

It was open. Inside the showroom were two remarkably fat girls. One had orange and silver hair cut to porcupine quills. She was dressed in a low-cut pinny with what looked like a skin-diver's wet-suit beneath it. The other had no hair at all but her scalp was painted like a rainbow target. She was wearing a medieval page-boy's outfit. Both of them had their faces made-up like chiefs of one of the more picturesque of the American Plains Indian tribes. They were far more riveting than any of the paintings on the wall but the pleasant girl receptionist at her desk near the door paid them scant attention. I could not resist and crept up close to them to overhear their conversation.

'No?' asked target-head.

'Possible,' nodded silver-thatch, 'but for the hall – or the loo. It would do for the loo.'

They sounded like ordinary human beings. London is certainly a wonderland to us country boys. The two moved slowly round the room, in perfect harmony spiritually if clashing horribly in colour, commenting on the paintings. They paused for a word with the girl at the desk and then went on out. I couldn't resist. I went up to her.

'Were they for real?' I asked her.

She smiled.

'Punks. Didn't you know they come from both ends of the social spectrum? One of those was a lady, an earl's daughter. They're starting a punk restaurant in Chelsea and they're looking for ornaments.'

'They *are* ornaments.'

She laughed appreciatively.

'I suppose so. I tried it once but it just seemed to me so unfeminine.'

'There's no substitute for an old-fashioned English rose.'

'Oh God, is that how you see me?'

'A sophisticated, old-fashioned English rose.'

'I suppose that'll have to do.'

'Tell me, the boy and the cheetah – what's the price?'

She looked alert and stood up.

'Oh, that's a very fine piece. Would you like to talk to Mr Dixon about it?'

I nodded brightly. I had decided to do a bright, fussy act.

'Yes, I'd love to. Or Mr Purdue.'

'Oh, there isn't any Mr Purdue. He was one of the original partners. But he only lasted a few months.'

'Goodness. I hope he didn't have a terrible accident?'

'Oh no. He just became a sleeping partner. He looks in quite often. He and Mr Dixon are still close friends which isn't always the case with ex-partners.'

'It's not, is it?'

'I'll get Mr Dixon.'

And she disappeared through a door at the rear of the

showroom. I posed myself in front of the Indian boy and cheetah with my hands on my chin, and an expression of deep concentration, blended with aesthetic reverence, on my face.

'Hello,' said a cheerful, well-bred voice at my elbow.

I turned, as if torn from reverie, to see a handsome, good-natured, well-groomed face beneath carefully-tended waves of silky brown hair.

This was a key moment. If this was indeed the face I had last seen almost obscured by the brim of a cloth cap next to a battered orange Mini in Bristol yesterday, then, although I might fail to recognise it, its owner would certainly recognise me. Maintaining a faint polite smile I studied the expression. Was there any hint of recognition, of concern, alarm? None, that I could detect. Either I meant nothing to Mr Dixon or he was a superb actor in splendid control of himself. No moustache, I noticed. But then moustaches can come and go. And the chin? Was it the chin from the Mini and the photograph? It was a chin. More than that, I could not be sure.

'Fine, isn't it?' said Dixon, nodding at the bronze figures.

'Very fine. Nineteenth century?'

'Eighteenth. And English, of course. It's by Ferdinand. Best known for the interiors of Platsworth and Stoneham Castle.'

'I must admit ——'

'No, he's not as well known as he should be. Except to serious collectors. I think most of them would now agree that he's the foremost exponent of the so-called Bath school.'

'Really? Bath? Perhaps that's what I sensed. I come from Bristol.'

'Do you? I know it well. Fine city.'

'We think so. Well now, I do like it. Yes, I think it might do very well. I have a spot for it in mind – in the main drawing room. Would it go with the Constable?'

'Perfectly.'

'How much is it?'

'Well, Ferdinand is on the upswing. Why don't you come

through to my office?'

'Certainly. Yes, it would certainly go in the West niche. At least I think it would. And even if it didn't – oh, what am I saying? That niche can be enlarged. Ferdinand? No, I can't say he's ever crossed my horizon.'

By this time, we were in a small but opulent office in which desk, chairs, bookcases and so on all looked like good pieces. Mr Dixon indicated a small armchair that was probably Louis something and I sat down in it and crossed my legs daintily.

'A drink, Mr ——?'

'Shoestring,' I said firmly but pleasantly, watching closely for a reaction. There was none that I detected. 'No, it's too early for me. Indeed, it's a month too early. I'm having six weeks on the wagon.'

'I admire your will-power. I find eight hours is about my abstinence limit. Well then, I'm glad you like the Ferdinand.'

'Oh, I do. But I should warn you straightaway that price *is* a consideration. Do you know I've just spent a week at a health farm and you simply wouldn't believe what it cost.'

'Really? Near Bristol? I know a place near there.'

'Do you? I wonder if it's the same one. This is a marvellous establishment. They have everything you can think of, including a heliport – is that right? Is that what they're called? And stables and squash courts and – well, just about everything.'

'It wouldn't be a place called Buttercups, would it?'

I gazed at him in simulated astonishment: 'Good heavens, do you know it?'

He smiled. All reactions absolutely normal.

'I've stayed there two – no three times, I think.'

'Well then, you must agree it's quite marvellous.'

'Yes, it – it certainly has the facilities.'

'You don't really vibrate with enthusiasm.'

'Oh, I don't know. I certainly wouldn't want to be over-critical. It's just that – well, the truth is there was something about the atmosphere that I found a bit – creepy.'

I sighed: 'It certainly is now – after what happened.'

He looked politely concerned and asked: 'Oh, what happened?'

'It was pretty ghastly. The manageress – a Miss Calderes ——'

At last, a reaction. His face suddenly lost its smile and went tense.

'Who?' he asked sharply.

'A Miss Calderes. Did you know her?'

'Yes. Yes, I did. She was the manageress when I was there, too.'

'Well, prepare yourself for a shock. She was murdered.'

He gazed at me in what had every appearance of being stupefaction.

'She was – what?'

'Oh heavens, it's too dreadful – she was found dead in the woods a few miles away. She'd been strangled.'

He gazed at me for a few seconds in complete silence and then he said softly: 'God.'

'You didn't read about it?'

He shook his head slowly.

'No.'

'There's been quite a lot in the paper.'

'I must have missed it. I ——'

He sat down slowly. He looked shattered.

'You seem very shocked.'

He glanced up at me.

'Mm? Yes, I – well, I knew her.'

'So you said. But of course everyone who stayed at Buttercups knew her. I believe she'd been there for years.'

'Yes she had,' he said quickly. 'Six years, I think it was.'

'Did you know her well?'

He pulled himself together.

'Well, as I said, I've been there – oh, God.'

'I say, there *is* something wrong?'

'Yes. The truth is – well, I had an affair with that girl. No, I really mustn't burden you with this.'

'Oh, I don't mind. As a matter of fact, I like burdens. I live alone so I'm endlessly nosy. If you want to talk about it. . . .'

He shook his head.

'No, I – I say, are they *sure* it was murder? It couldn't have been suicide?'

'Good Lord, no. People can't strangle themselves.'

'I suppose not. Well, that's something.'

'I beg your pardon?'

'No, I'm sorry. That must sound heartless. The fact is, I have several reasons to feel guilty about Maria Calderes.'

'Guilty? That doesn't seem likely.'

'Doesn't it? I seduced her. I got bored. She was the prettiest girl in the place. I like girls. And – I seduced her.'

'Well, she was a grown woman ——'

'Yes, but damn it, she was a virtuous one! I know she was from what she told me and from her resistance. But I gave her the full treatment – flowers, declarations, everything – and in the end I – had an affair with her.'

'I don't suppose you were the first.'

'Perhaps not – but she wasn't promiscuous. Anyway, that's not the worst.'

'Oh? You weren't the father of her child, were you?'

His expression changed. Amazement and anger chased each other across it. He half rose——

'What the hell do you mean? Why do you say that?'

I smiled innocently.

'Well, in spite of pills and things, babies do sometimes still result from affairs, don't they?'

He sat down again with a sigh. He made a gesture of dismissal.

'I suppose so. No, no, I wasn't the father of her child. But I – could have been ——'

'I beg your pardon?'

'Well, stepfather, anyway. About two months after we'd – after our affair – she suddenly turned up at my flat – here in London. She said that – oh, something about the Home Office wanting to deport her and she had to marry an Englishman. Then she could bring her child over here. I think that was it. Anyway, I refused point blank.'

'It was a lot to ask.'

'Was it? I don't know. Men have done it before to help women. She didn't want anything else from me. She even offered to pay. I wasn't having any part of it.'

'Why not?'

'Pure bloody selfishness. I – well, I've got an understanding with a girl. Actually, she's an earl's daughter. She's not at all illiberal but I don't think she'd be too keen on being wife number two, if you see what I mean.'

'Well, of course. Was Miss Calderes very upset?'

'Yes. No. She was upset but very controlled. She apologised for asking and left. Funny, it was all so formal and a few months before we'd been – well, pretty informal.'

'How long ago was that?'

'Oh, five or six months – something like ——'

'And you haven't seen her since?'

'No. God, how rotten.'

'You'll probably have the police round, you know.'

He glanced at me. He said listlessly:

'Really?'

'Well, someone at Buttercups must have seen you together. It'll reach the police sooner or later and I should think they'll want to interview you.'

'I suppose so. Perhaps I can help them. I suppose I'd better contact them, hadn't I?'

'I should think they'd appreciate it.'

He nodded.

'I will.'

I glanced at my watch.

'Good heavens, my train. Could we perhaps talk about the Barnado – was it a Barnado ——?'

'Hm? Oh, you mean the Ferdinand. Yes, of course. Well, as I said, it *is* a good piece and its price is set accordingly. We're asking eight thousand, Mr Shoelace.'

'Shoestring,' I said reproachfully.

I went over and over it in my mind on the train back to Bristol. I couldn't fault him. His innocence had been convincing. Too convincing? Not really. Innocent people behave innocently. And only the cleverest of guilty people are capable of that. Besides, his art gallery was clearly doing well. Why should a personable, sensitive, successful young man go around killing people? Even if he was well paid for it, he could probably earn as much by shifting a couple of Barnados – or Ferdinands – before lunch. Well, a Ferdinand would arrive at the house in the next day or two. Mr Dixon had been perfectly happy for me to have it on approval for a few days, provided I paid the expenses of transport and insurance. Don wouldn't be overjoyed by the sums he'd mentioned but I was very curious to see if it would arrive in a short-wheelbase black or dark blue Bedford van. Would he go to the police? That too would be a significant factor. Mr Dixon might – he just might – be a supercool killer but I didn't think so. Even if he was, what possible reason could he have had for murdering Maria Calderes? Had she found out some guilty truth about him? Had she been blackmailing him? To ask those questions was to answer them. The girl I had met on two occasions would have been incapable of blackmail. And if she'd known anything terrible about someone, she'd have gone to the police, even at the risk of giving away things about herself she didn't want known. Perhaps Dixon had been the man in the orange Mini but I could not connect him in my mind with the strangler of Maria Calderes. Still, there was one more step I could take that just might expose him. It was a long shot but I felt the time had come to make the acquaintance of the wealthy Mr Cranston, the owner of a health farm and den of iniquity called Buttercups.

But I reached Bristol too late and too tired for a trip out to the place that evening. Instead, I checked in at Radio West and went through the tapes which didn't contain anything that needed immediate attention. Then I drove down to The Blackmore.

'Hope you didn't stop too much flak, Albert?' I said sympathetically.

'How do you mean, Eddie?'

'Well – about anything – getting me that photostat, for

129

instance.'

'Oh, that? No, no problem.'

'How's the investigation going?'

'Can I get you a drink, Eddie?'

'Hm? Oh, sorry. My round, I think,' and to the barman, 'A pint of Guinness, please, and a large Scotch and soda.'

'What did you ask me, Eddie?'

'How is the good Super doing?'

'We've traced her to London.'

I felt a cold thrill at this.

'Maria Calderes? A positive identification?'

'Right. Two passengers on the train – not together. They both placed her getting off at Paddington.'

'I see.'

I saw what I didn't want to see. Maria Calderes going to see the bright, personable young art dealer and returning to the Bristol district in the back of a van.

'Well, in that case, Albert, I'd better tell you. The fellow I've been to see – he knew her.'

'How do you mean, Eddie?'

'They had an affair. He admitted it. At Buttercups. I figure he's clean but – you deserve the facts. The only thing is, how can you inform the Super without admitting that you got me that photostat?'

'I'll think of a way, Eddie.'

'Anything else, Albert?'

'Not really.'

'What about the Mant – the barman? Is he still with us?'

'Still alive, you mean?'

'Yes.'

'He's still breathing. They think he'll pull through. But he could be a vegetable.'

'God. Have you been putting the heat on Cranston?'

'Who?'

'Cranston. The boss of Buttercups. He's behind it.'

'Officially, it's a hit-and-run, Eddie. We can't put the heat on anyone without a grain of evidence.'

'I told you. That barman was writing a book exposing

Cranston's nasty little ways.'

'Yes, but we only have your word for that, Eddie. And you're under suspicion of murder.'

'Well, *I* can put the heat on Cranston. And I intend to – tomorrow morning.'

'What do you plan doing?'

'Having a chat with him.'

'At Buttercups?'

'Assuming that's where he is, yes.'

'If you go there, you'll be trespassing, Eddie.'

'You could be right, Albert.'

'They could phone us and I might have to come out and arrest you.'

'Well, if you do, Albert, use my other arm, will you? I've still got grooves in this one.'

And I waved the arm he had toyed with several times recently. He grinned.

'Sorry about that, Eddie. But I'm in a difficult position. I'd be drummed out of the force if they knew I was feeding you tips.'

'I know that, Albert, and I do appreciate your efforts. How about a large, lovely foaming pint?'

'I won't say no, Eddie.'

'Thank God for that. The shock would unnerve me.'

'How do you mean?'

'Nothing, Albert. Another pint of Guinness, please.'

I drove home, feeling a bit low. If Dixon proved to be the killer, the police would certainly zero in on him before I could. Indeed, there seemed nothing more I could usefully do in that direction. Oh, I'd get a couple of good and exciting programmes out of it but it wouldn't be the same as bringing in the murderer myself. But, was he? It didn't add up. There were missing factors. Maybe there were several assassins on the loose? Maybe Dixon was the private hit-man of Buttercups but had nothing to do with Maria Calderes' death? Yes, but he'd known her. Well, what did that prove?

When I got back to the house, I played the Ansaphone.

There was a long and complicated message from Jill and Stu, two boring friends of Erica's, but nothing from Erica herself, nothing from the Philippines. Well, it didn't matter that much. She'd have done what I wanted her to do. I toyed with the idea of going out for a meal. But no, if Erica did relent and phone through, I should be there to take the call. I went into the kitchen and found a plate of decaying veal in the fridge and some tins of rice pudding. Mentally reproaching Erica with her choice of iron rations, I opened the rice pudding and ate it. It tasted so foul that I had a large whisky to wash away the taste. The whisky tasted so good that I had another one to preserve the taste. At this point, a kind of chain reaction set in and I was on my seventh large whisky when, at about midnight Bristol time, the phone rang. I located the instrument with very little trouble and answered it.

'Hello?'

'Eddie, is that you?'

'Erica, thank God you've called.'

'What do you mean?'

'I mean – I was afraid you wouldn't call. But now you have, so I'm not afraid any longer.'

'Are you drunk again?'

'Drunk again? What rot. Perish the thought.'

'You are. I'm going to hang up.'

'Erica! Just – now listen. I'm not drunk, not a bit drunk. I've had one large whisky and a very fatiguing day. So – so – please deliver your report.'

'What?'

'I would be grateful if you would tell me what you've discovered.'

'Well ——' she sounded dubious. I heard a deep sigh, then she resumed. 'All right. It's not much.'

And she gave me a short account of what she had been doing. She hadn't got far before I exclaimed: 'That's it!'

'What?'

'I've got it. I've got it. I've got it.'

'Got what?'

'It. The clue. A clue. Of course. Of course. That's why she said that.'

'Said what? Who? What are you talking about?'

'Erica, listen. I can't explain now. Too long – too expensive. Don't be cross. But you've done fine. You've done just fine. Now – when are you coming back?'

'Tomorrow. Didn't you get my message?'

'Yes. I did. Got your message. Okay, come back tomorrow. But just one last little thing. Very important. Could be conclusive. Go to the local police department and ——'

And I gave her detailed instructions. After a certain amount of grumbling, Erica agreed to do as I instructed. Then I hung up. Then I looked at my watch. Then I shook my head. No, too late. It wouldn't do to frighten the boy. But first thing in the morning – first thing!

And then I had another large whisky to celebrate. I was right and the Super was wrong. I knew now why Maria Calderes had lied. Erica had helped me to find what it was Maria had said to me in the car that had been significant. Oh yes, it was significant all right. And the case would soon be solved.

At which point, thinking of Mrs Sweet's nerves, I heaved myself up off the floor and staggered upstairs to Erica's room where I slept long and deep.

Chapter 8

I woke up with only a slight hangover. What time was it? Half-past ten. Damn! Why didn't the bloody alarm clock ever work? I seized the instrument vengefully and found that I hadn't wound it. Damn! There was a lot to do. I hadn't time for the water and walking routine so I contented myself with three cups of coffee and three aspirins. Then I set off for the house of Jean Cole, the Filipino with the unlikely name.

When I got to the quiet suburban street and parked the car, I felt a sudden sense of dismay. The FOR SALE sign in front of the house now had a band pasted across it reading SOLD. I got out of the car and went up to the front door and rang the bell. There was no answer. I hadn't expected one but, for form's sake, I rang again. No answer. I stepped on to the small front lawn and approached the bay window. It was made of alternate panes of bubble-glass and very dirty clear glass. It was hard to see inside but, as far as I could make out, the room was empty. There was no furniture and, I thought, no carpet on the floor. I walked round the house and peered in every room that was accessible. The same, no furniture. But through a pane in the side door, I saw several cases in the hall. So, the place wasn't entirely abandoned. Presumably, someone would be coming for those cases. Would I have to mount a stake-out and spend hours or possibly days outside the house? The idea didn't appeal to me.

I went to the front door of the neighbouring house to the left and rang. There was no answer. I transferred my attentions to the house to the right and rang there. There was no answer but, from the corner of my eye, I caught that flicker of a gauze curtain that always betrays neighbourly concern. Right, I could play it that way. I pressed my finger on the bell and simply hung on. She either had stamina or cloth ears because it must have been ringing, quite audibly to me, for about two minutes before the door suddenly opened and a little old lady with a sweet face but, as I was soon to discover, a rotten nature, stood there.

'Leave off ringing,' she urged harshly. 'Good mind to call the police.'

'I am the police – or the next best thing. We're trying to locate Mrs Cole.'

'Who?'

'The lady next door.'

She sniffed.

'*Mrs* Cole! She isn't any missus. Not any lady, either – some of the carry-ons.'

'Do you know her?'

'Not any more than I can help. She's gone, any rate. House is sold.'

'So I see. Do you happen to know where she's gone?'

'Down, I shouldn't wonder. Straight down. Best place for the likes of her.'

'How charitable. You didn't get on?'

'Never could abide foreigners. Specially them with slant eyes. This was an English street until she come to it.'

'Well, never mind, perhaps it will be again.'

'Anything else?'

'No, thank you. You've been most helpful.'

She made an irate sound and closed the door in my face. There were one or two more questions I would have put to her but I'd seen something that might make it unnecessary. A car had pulled up behind mine and a fat man had emerged from the back. The driver stayed in his place. It was obviously a minicab. I stayed where I was, watching covertly as the fat man waddled up the path of Jean Cole's nearly-empty house, inserted a key in the lock and went in. He left the front door ajar in order, I assumed, to make it easier to bring out the cases. I moved quickly across the

135

path beside the front door of the house I was at, crossed a low wooden fence, and hurried to Jean Cole's front door. I entered. The little fat man was just approaching me with a suitcase in either hand. He was sufficiently surprised or shocked by my entrance to drop the two cases with a thump. I grinned amiably.

'What's going on? Where's Jean?' I asked.

'There's no one here,' he said with, as far as I could judge, a southern-American accent. 'The place is empty.'

'I can see that. But ——' I winked at him broadly. 'I'm one of Jean's regulars. She opening up somewhere else?'

He considered me for a while with an impassive expression on his chubby features. Then he grinned suddenly.

'She's gone, boy. She's left this town for good.'

'That so?' I said. 'Where's she setting up shop?'

He picked up his cases again.

'You better just forget her, boy. You won't see her again.'

I pushed the front door shut behind me with my heel. He put his cases down again. He asked:

'Are you a thief, boy?'

'No. Are you?'

'No way. I'm just collecting some property belonging to Mrs Cole.'

'Why?'

'I don't reckon that's any of your business. Now just kindly open that door.'

'No way. Not until you tell me where I can find her.'

'I'm not going to do that.'

'I think you are.'

He studied me impassively for a moment. Then he grinned his broad grin again.

'Hell, boy, why not? Have you got a pen?'

'Sure have,' I said, mimicking him faintly.

I reached into my breast pocket, pulled out a ballpoint and held it out to him. It was a mistake. My arm was seized with a grip at least equal to that of DC Pelham's and I found myself secured in a painful half-Nelson.

'I wasn't a bouncer for nothing, boy,' he said solemnly.

'I may be small but I'm strong.'

'Point taken,' I gasped. 'Now, please let go.'

'Who are you?' he asked curiously.

'Eddie Shoestring.'

'Thought you might be. Jean's talked about you.'

'On the transatlantic telephone?'

'That's right and here in Bristol.'

'Could you let me go?'

'No problem. But I don't aim to. Just yet. What do you want with Jean?'

'I just want to talk to her.'

'What about?'

'About Johnny.'

'That's what I figured. Now listen, boy, and listen good. Jean and I are leaving for the States just as soon as she's got her visa fixed. We don't want any trouble.'

'There won't be any. I give you my word. But if she doesn't talk to me she'll have to talk to the police.'

He unexpectedly released my arm.

'I love Jean,' he confessed. 'I aim to marry her.'

'That's fine by me. Are you from Mississippi by any chance?'

'I am.'

'And you're really going to marry Jean?'

'I am. And I know she's a whore, if that's what you mean. It doesn't bother me because I'm in the brothel business. I reckon Jean'll be a fine wife for me. And she'll be a novelty in Mississippi. We don't get many Oriental gals there.'

'When did you meet her?'

'You guessed right, boy. About five months ago.'

'And it was love at first night, if I can put it like that?'

'Pretty much.'

'And that left the problem of Johnny, didn't it?'

'Right, boy. I see you've worked it out.'

'I have. Now, can I see her?'

He gave me his long impassive stare again. Then he grinned again.

'Well, I don't see how I can stop you other than kill you and I just never do kill people. But you promise you won't go to the police? Leastways, not till you've spoken to her?'

'I promise and – I don't see why they need ever know.'

He smiled and said, 'Well, let's see – she and Johnny are up in London at the embassy today. Come tomorrow to our hotel. Say about noon. It's the Bristol Palace.'

He once more picked up his cases.

'Look, I don't want my arm twisted again. But how do I know you'll be there?'

He put his cases down again.

'You think of everything, don't you, boy?'

He reached into his inside pocket. I felt a spurt of alarm. Was he going to pull out a gun? It turned out to be a passport.

'Copy the number down, boy,' he invited me. 'Then you'll be able to get on my tail. But I'll be there. I've got nothing to hide.'

'I believe you,' I said, but I copied down his passport number.

Then he picked up his cases yet again. I held the door for him and we departed.

I drove straight to the Public Record Office and did some checking. Then I drove to Buttercups. I got there as the Maharanee was being wheeled jabbering out of the main house. From the heliport, about a quarter of a mile away, came the thudding of a helicopter warming up. The Maharanee had her usual escort of doctors and nurses and, in addition, a tall, bronzed man a little too stout to look healthy. He was watching the procession with a proprietorial air. I approached him:

'Not so much losing a client – more gaining peace of mind, eh?' I said cheerfully.

He frowned at me.

'Who are you?' he asked curtly.

'Eddie Shoestring. You've been losing a lot of staff recently.'

'I think you may be trespassing, Mr Shoestring. I may

have to have you removed.'

'You're good at that, aren't you, Mr Cranston?'

'Yes, I am. You've been here before – uninvited. I'd advise you to go away and stay away.'

'And if I don't?'

'Well, I could have you thrown out.' He looked at me contemptuously. 'I could probably throw you out myself.'

'Where's the Maharanee going?' I asked cheerfully.

'I don't know. She's insane. She comes for a week and then goes. I suspect she does the rounds of all the health farms. I suspect that that is the method her family use to keep her quiet.'

'I hope she hasn't left her emeralds behind.'

'So do I. And if you're implying that I'm a jewel thief, Mr Shoestring, you're being idiotic.'

We watched the cortège moving slowly towards the heliport. Every so often the Maharanee leaned out of her chair and took a swipe at one of her keepers.

'Why did you try to kill the Mantis?' I asked amiably.

He looked at me sharply.

'Try to kill who?'

'The funny little fellow that worked here as receptionist for a time.'

'I don't know what you're talking about. And I haven't tried to kill anyone for decades, Mr Shoestring.'

'I don't suppose you have. Personally. You give the orders and other people do the killing.'

'What an offensive chap you are. Scruffy, too. I think I will have you thrown out.'

'I think I know why you tried to kill the Mantis.'

The Maharanee's party had reached the heliport. I noticed that her big Rolls Royce was no longer on the patio. Perhaps she couldn't stand the bumps. The thump of the helicopter built to a whine. Two white-coated figures were now hoisting the Maharanee's wheelchair into the machine. Cranston was concentrating on the scene. I went on: 'The Mantis was investigating you, Cranston.'

'Really?' he asked indifferently. 'Do you know, people are

always investigating me. I don't think I'd feel comfortable if a few people weren't investigating me.'

'Have you been a gangster all your life?'

'I'm not a gangster, Mr Shoestring. I'm a businessman.'

'There's business and business.'

'True. And do you know something, Mr Shoestring? Any business that's profitable cuts corners. In a sense all business-men are gangsters. The gangster is simply someone who eliminates the tedious business of manufacturing, distribut-ing and book-keeping.'

'Like you?'

He sighed.

'No, I have to run this place for my sins.'

'I believe you do very well?'

He nodded.

'Yes, I do. Very well.'

'All from this health farm?'

'No, I have other business interests.'

'Like the Royal Fountain Hotel in Bath?'

This produced some effect. He darted a sharp glance at me.

'Yes.'

'And like The Trencherman Restaurant in Bristol?'

'It seems you've been investigating, too, Mr Shoestring. Well, you seem to have discovered that I have a wide range of legitimate business interests.'

'A wide range, yes. Legitimate, no. That's what the Mantis was doing. Accumulating evidence of your illegal activities. That's why he worked in your establishments one after another. He was writing a book about you.'

'Really?' he smiled wolfishly. 'And just who did you say this person was?'

'The person that was hit by an orange Mini in Bristol the day before yesterday.'

'Oh, that person. Mr Shoestring, I have no idea what you're talking about. But if you're suggesting that I was involved in some road accident in Bristol then you'd better tell the police about it.'

'I have done. They've got it down as a hit-and-run.'

'Well, why don't you do the same? If you keep pestering me I shall have to have you thrown out.'

'It wouldn't look good. Only a handful of your clients are gangsters. The rest would be shocked by strong-arm stuff.'

He nodded thoughtfully.

'You have a point. But don't push your luck too far.'

'How far did Maria Calderes push hers?'

He didn't say anything. We both watched the little cluster of people around the distant helicopter draw back. The whine of the engine increased. The machine rocked slightly and then lifted with its cargo of a deranged plutocrat. We watched it swing gently in the air, lean over and then curve away in the direction of Bristol. Cranston sighed faintly.

'Come into my office, Mr Shoestring. I might even offer you a drink.'

I followed him through two sets of swinging green-baize doors and finally into what seemed more like a well-appointed drawing room than an office. It did have a small desk near one wall but Cranston waved me towards an armchair beside the ornate marble fireplace.

'Scotch and soda?' he asked.

'Please,' I replied.

I remained silent while he opened a small bar in what looked like an antique Chesterfield and fixed the drinks. Then he came over to the fireplace, handed me mine and sat down opposite me. He held up his glass:

'Cheers!' he said.

We drank. Then he said earnestly:

'I'll give you a thousand pounds if you find the murderer of Maria Calderes.'

'How about Dixon?'

I said it sharply. I said 'Dixon' loudly. I watched narrowly for any hint of a reaction. I detected none.

'Who?' he asked.

'Mr Dixon of London Town. The art dealer.'

'Art dealer? Yes – I know him. He's stayed here – several times, I believe. Why should he have killed my manageress?'

'You tell me.'

He stood up. I could see that he was angry. I could also see that his anger was a formidable thing.

'Get out, Mr Shoestring. Get off Buttercups within ten minutes or I'll have you beaten up.'

'So you do have men beaten up?'

'Yes, when they're trespassers and I have a perfect right to. Now, go.'

I hadn't moved.

'All right,' I said, in a conciliatory voice. 'I believe you. Why do *you* think Maria Calderes was killed?'

He looked at me with a hard expression for a moment. Then he shook his head and sat down again. Behind him, through an open window, I saw two obese ladies playing tennis.

'I've no idea. I've no idea why anyone should have felt the slightest animosity towards her. She was a very fine human being.'

It was like hearing a hawk praising a thrush but I believed him.

'She'd been here a long time, I believe?' I asked.

'Six years. She was excellent, efficient, thoughtful, always ready to work overtime. Everyone liked her.'

'Where did you find her?'

'She was working in a hotel – the Royal Fountain, as a matter of fact. I'd just bought it and I was staying there for a week to get things running smoothly. She was only a maid but I spotted that – well, she had qualities. I transferred her to Buttercups with a view to making her manageress and that's what I did.'

It all sounded convincing and it all tied in with what I already knew.

'Was she promiscuous?' I asked.

He shook his head with a fastidious expression.

'You people do have grubby little minds, don't you?'

'It's a grubby little world, Mr Cranston. Much of it, anyway. Mr Dixon, the art dealer, claimed that he had an affair with her.'

142

Cranston shrugged.

'Possible, I suppose. I'm only here about three months in the year. I can't watch everything. But Maria was certainly not promiscuous. Why do you imagine this – this art dealer should have killed her?'

I shook my head.

'I don't. It's just a possibility. Why did you offer me a thousand pounds to find the killer?'

'Because I want him caught. Because I had great respect for Maria Calderes.' He paused and then he smiled his unpleasant smile. 'Because I like people to know that I take care of my interests.'

'The way you took care of the Mantis? It was a waste of time, you know. I've got the book.'

'The book?' he asked politely.

'The one the Mantis was writing. I intend to hand it to the police. It's got enough detail in it to put you away for several years.'

'How disagreeable. I'll tell you what: don't give it to the police. Publish it. And we'll split the royalties.'

'You don't believe I've got it? Phone your hit-man. He'll tell you that he's only got one notebook. I've got the other three. The Mantis thought something unpleasant might be in store for him and he asked me to hang on to his work.'

'I see. Well then, run along, Mr Shoestring, and take it to the police. Whatever it is you're talking about. But to more serious matters. I meant what I said. If you find the murderer of Maria Calderes, I'll pay you a thousand pounds. If you come back here for any reason other than to tell me that you've found her, I'll set the dogs on you.'

He rose. His smile was steely. I rose too. I didn't extend my hand. Somehow I didn't think he'd welcome any such gesture. Moreover, like everyone else I'd been meeting lately, he might seize my hand and give it a twist or two. He might even twist it off. I had him down as a man who'd order an execution without the least remorse. But I didn't think he'd had anything to do with the murder of Maria Calderes or been involved in criminal dealings with Mr

Dixon, the art dealer.

He escorted me to the main hall where a large, one-legged man swung eagerly towards him on crutches.

'Goodbye, Mr Shoestring,' he said, before turning his attention to his mutilated client.

I went out on to the patio. The standards of the place seemed to be slipping. There were only two Rolls Royces out there now and several lesser makes. My Cortina didn't look so conspicuous.

As I drove slowly up the magnificent avenue of limes towards the woods, I brooded on the interview. I was sure that Cranston had been responsible for the attack by mini-car on the Mantis. I was also sure that he had the Mantis's manuscript in his possession or at least knew where it was. Otherwise he'd have taken more interest in my claim to have it. Perhaps it was already destroyed? But I doubted that. People are such egotists. Cranston would have wanted to read it. Crooks are even more keen to read about their crooked exploits than politicians are. That notebook – and there was only one, I suspected, not three as I'd made out – was still in existence somewhere.

I reached the woods and drove through them slowly, passing an ancient Daimler going the other way. I reached the unmade-up stretch of road and started bumping over it. I saw him almost at once. He was standing by the Butter-cups sign gazing gloomily at the rutted track. Beside him was his motorcycle with the giveaway speaker and box on the pillion. He was a despatch rider.

As he got on his bike and started the engine, I drew level with him. I stopped and rolled down the offside window. Leaning over, I said: 'Anything wrong?'

He shook his head glumly.

'They never told me you had to be rally-trained for this job. How far is the place, anyway?'

'Buttercups? It's about two miles.'

'And is the road all like this bit?'

'No, no, only the first mile or so. I'm having it made up later in the year. Personally, I prefer the unspoiled appearance but some of my guests have complained.'

'Are you the governor, then?'

'That's right, Charles Cranston. I suppose you've got something for one of my guests?'

'No, for you.'

'Really? Then you're in luck. You won't have to brave the rutted trail.'

'Thank God for that.'

He stopped his engine and went to the rear of his bike. He opened the despatch box and took out a package. My heart jumped and a thrill went through me. It was a flat rectangle, just the size of the notebook I had last seen in the hands of the Mantis in the restaurant in Bath. He approached me with it, first holding out a clipboard.

'Sign, please,' he ordered.

'Certainly.'

I took the clipboard and illegally wrote Charles Cranston in my own hand. The driver wouldn't know the difference. He handed me the packet. I put it negligently on the seat beside me.

'Doubtless my accountant's report,' I said in a tone of disgust. 'Frankly, I wish I'd never met you.'

He grinned.

'Sorry, mate. Can't say the same. You've saved me a bouncing.'

'Right. Goodbye then.'

And I started my engine and drove off. I waited some time for him to pass me on the road back to Bristol but he didn't. I thereupon stopped the car and wrote down his licence number, although I didn't think it would prove to be of much help. Then I opened the packet. Bull's eye! It was the Mantis's book all right.

Where could I go to read it? Home? Not good. It was just possible that Cranston would get on my trail quickly. I didn't want any visits from hit men while I was peacefully reading. The station? There might be a lot of hassle and very little peace there. Besides, if Cranston was really determined, he'd send his torpedoes into the sacred premises of

F

Radio West. I settled for my boat. It wasn't as secret as the lair of the Yeti but not many people in Bristol knew about it. Besides it was such a pleasant day and the boatyard was such a haven of peace. I drove down there. The sun sparkled on the oily swell of the harbour. I bought myself two hamburgers and a bottle of coke from Joe, the West Indian who catered to the needs of us boat-owners. Then I clambered over the side of the rotting wreck which, were it ever launched, would doubtless sink like a stone, and repaired to the cabin. There I stretched out on the bunk and started to read.

It was a loser. The Mantis hadn't just been odd. He'd been a fully-freaked-out religious nut. The story *might* have been about a crook called Charles Cranston and his nefarious activities or it might have been about Lucifer getting slung out of heaven. It was written in such a weird, allegorical style you could hardly tell. Cranston, if it was indeed meant to be Cranston, was referred to as 'The Evil One'. The story was told in the following way: 'Then the Evil One schemed to extend his nefarious dominion. Plotting with brothers in infamy, he secured stores intended for benign ends and perverted them, by way of corrupt manipulation, to the increase of his worldly possessions.'

It contained about as much hard evidence as the inside of a light bulb. And he'd been murdered, or nearly murdered, for that? Poor, bloody, innocent half-wit. His manuscript would have no value as evidence. Or precious little. Perhaps the police could dig a few incriminating facts out of it, but ——

But – and the big idea lit up beautifully in my mind – Cranston didn't know what the manuscript contained! He'd have merely given instructions that it was to be delivered to him and if his strong-arm had taken a look at the contents he wouldn't, since strong-arms never have strong heads, have been able to make head or tail of it.

I leaped off my bunk, bounded from my boat and drove straight to Bristol Central. There, I spent a cordial and instructive half-hour with Superintendent Bowen. Then I drove to the station and, a quarter of an hour after I'd explained the scheme to Don, and as soon as the news and Recipe of the Day were finished, a Shoestring Special was on the air.

'Hello, listeners. Eddie Shoestring here. I'm sorry if I'm about to spoil anyone's after-lunch nap but I know a lot of you are wondering how I'm making out in my fight to clear my name and nail the murderer of Maria Calderes. And, fans, this is coming to you live, as I promised you my reports would. The first thing to be said is that I'm closing in. I can't name the murderer today because I don't yet know his name but I have in my possession something which is going to supply the missing clue. I have in my possession a manuscript notebook that was written by a man who was the victim of an assassination attempt in Bristol the day before yesterday. They tried to silence him for the oldest and sickest of all underworld reasons: because he knew too much. And they may have succeeded because, at this moment, the man is lying desperately ill in the intensive care unit of Bristol Royal Infirmary. He may survive but doctors are doubtful if he will ever give testimony in court. They expect that, if he does pull through, his brain will have been so badly damaged that he will only be a living vegetable. However, before he was attacked this man filled a large notebook with an account of the criminal activities he had observed. Where? Well, fans, as you know one of the big problems with a programme of this kind is the law of libel. Radio West has to make sure that it doesn't ever put out anything questionable. But – and this is big – I am so confident of my information, so certain of its reliability, that I am going to name names. Usually, I have to use pseudonyms and other devices to make sure we are protected from libel actions but here are two verifiable names for you: Buttercups and Charles Cranston. What is Buttercups? Who is Charles Cranston? Buttercups, as some of you may already know, is a large establishment about twelve miles outside Bristol which pretends to be a health farm. That's not quite accurate because it really is a health farm and a lot of its clients are innocent people who merely visit it for reasons of health. But Buttercups is more than that. It is a meeting place for thieves and criminals but not petty thieves and minor criminals. Oh no. Buttercups is the resort of the big boys. There, they plan their illegal operations. Drugs, gambling, prostitution – yes, and assassination – are all planned and organised at Buttercups. And Charles Cranston is the King Crook, the man who presides over Buttercups and is himself up to his sticky fingers in crime. What crime? It's a juicy list. Some of the villainies specified in the manuscript I have in my possession are ———'

And I went on to give a few examples of Cranston's bent activities. I didn't give many and I didn't make too much of the ones I did give. The reason, of course, is that I had no hard evidence. I was basing it on long-standing police suspicions which the good Superintendent had revealed to me. It was a try-on. The police had never been able to secure proof that would stand up in court but they were pretty sure of their information. Cranston was a smart operator who covered his tracks but he would be very upset to think that I had a document giving chapter and verse about his rackets in my possession. And now I had to persuade him that the vital evidence *was* in my possession and not already in the hands of the police. I continued:

'When the time comes, fans, I will hand this manuscript to the police. But the time has not come yet. Why not? Because as far as I am concerned, Cranston's criminal career is not the main issue. The main issue is the murder of Maria Calderes and, as you know, I am, and I remain, the chief suspect. If I don't clear my name, I just could hear a judge inviting me to spend the next fifteen years as the guest of the crown. Now, in addition to information about Cranston and Buttercups, the book I have in my possession contains certain leads that will, I hope, put me straight on the track of the murderer. I intend to check these out. Don't forget, I'm competing with the police. I've staked my reputation on bringing in the murderer before they do and this manuscript will help me to do that. I'm signing off now because I've got a lot of detecting to do in the next few days. But it won't be long before you'll be hearing from Eddie Shoestring again. And when you do, you'll probably also hear the name of the man who murdered Maria Calderes. Keep listening!'

Half an hour. That was the amount of time that the Superintendent and I had agreed on. I'd get home exactly half an hour after the broadcast. And then – well, then it was all set up and should go as smoothly as a blonde in a bubble-bath. And if it didn't? Well, of course, if it didn't, Eddie Shoestring might wind up with a few dents in the old frame – or even worse. Yes, but the police knew what they were doing. Didn't they? I tried not to think of some of the appalling cock-ups I'd heard about or even had personal experience of. Sometimes squads of police charged into the wrong house. Sometimes they had premises under heavy observation while fearsome crimes were committed inside. Sometimes they were late. Sometimes – steady on, Shoestring. The Superintendent knows what's at risk. He'll put one of his smartest chaps on it. You're in no danger.

Then I began to worry about the other hazard. Suppose no one – or none of the right people – had heard my broadcast? Suppose Cranston didn't even know it had taken place? No, that wasn't likely. His coverage was good. His network of informants was far-flung. Someone would have tipped him off. Wouldn't they?

By the time I reached the front door I was near hoping that Cranston hadn't got the message. Courage, Shoestring, I whispered to myself – and unlocked the door. I entered. I paused in the hall and listened. There was no sound in the house. I shut the door noisily. I walked along the hall and entered the front living-room. And then I knew that they were there all right. I didn't see anyone but the room looked as if a hurricane had blown through it. All the furniture was overturned and much of it was slashed and dismembered. I gulped at this and to my credit I was thinking of Erica. She was fond of her furniture. She wouldn't be happy at the fate that had befallen it. All drawers had been pulled from their frames and emptied promiscuously in a heap. Papers were scattered everywhere. Vases had been smashed. It was an utter, disastrous mess.

'Christ!' I exclaimed loudly and I turned quickly as if about to bolt for the front door. And there they were, two of them, between me and it. I wondered briefly where they'd been hiding. In the broom cupboard, probably. They'd heard my car pull up, as I'd intended.

'Oh, hello,' I said, studying the chin of the taller of the two men as I backed into the raped living room. 'There's no money in the house.'

I observed that they were advancing towards me. As soon as I had cleared the living-room door, I grabbed it and tried to slam it in their faces. They both hurled themselves at the door, as I'd assumed they would, and pushed it open, sending me staggering back across the room. I held out my hands as if to ward them off.

'Now look, fellows,' I said ingratiatingly. 'I've got about fifteen, twenty quid on me. You're welcome to that but I'd be grateful if you didn't smash up any more of the furniture. It has sentimental value.'

I fished out my wallet with what I hoped would look like desperation and started extracting the money. The shorter of the two kicked the door shut behind him and the other – the one with the familiar chin (or was it?) – advanced on me and knocked the wallet out of my hand. Where had the police hidden the bug? Had the goons found it? Was that why I was making all the running with the dialogue? The chin (yes, it was! I was sure – and the moustache was right too) suddenly said: 'We want the book, Shoestring.'

So they hadn't found the bug! Assuming the police had planted it. Oh God, let the police not botch this one. I don't want to join the Mantis in intensive care.

'Book?' I said in feigned astonishment. 'Haven't you fellows ever heard of public libraries? Frankly this is ridiculous.'

'*The* book. You know which book.'

What kind of accent? Not Bristol and not London. South coast perhaps. Oh well, we could analyse it from the tape.

Oh God, let there be a tape. Let the police be near and listening.

'Oh?' I exclaimed. 'Are you fans? Have you been listening to my little programme?'

'Let's kick him,' suggested the shorter of the two, more I felt to stake a claim in the conversation than because he felt it was a sound idea. But the Chin seemed to think the notion had merit.

'We'll kick him – if we have to. Shoestring, do you want to be kicked? Hard? And often?'

'No. I'd do almost anything to avoid it.'

'Then give us the book.'

'I can't.'

'We'll have to kick him,' asserted the shorter with surly enthusiasm.

'Hang on!' I pleaded. 'It's not here. And it's no good kicking me because I don't know where it is.'

The Chin shook his head sadly.

'Don't expect us to believe that, do you?'

'Yes, because if you think about it, I'd be crazy to have it in my possession. I knew Cranston would send someone for it. You're just quicker off the mark than I'd expected. Now, I'll make *you* an offer. How much does Cranston pay you?'

'None of your business,' grunted the kicking enthusiast.

'I'll double it,' I said quickly. 'Don't worry. Radio West will pay. All you have to do is to supply a little information.'

'The thing is,' said the Chin, and then uttered the words I was praying for, assuming a tape was running somewhere, 'Mr Cranston doesn't like people to double-cross him. He might send some other people to kick us. And we don't like being kicked, do we, Ned?'

The other contented himself with a grunt.

'All right,' I said. 'I admire your loyalty. But the book isn't here and I don't know where it is.'

'It may not be here,' said the Chin, solemnly, 'but you must know where it is.'

'No, I don't,' I said, 'because – because ——' and I tried

151

hard to give the impression of a man desperately trying to think up a convincing lie.

'Let's start kicking him,' said the shorter.

They advanced on me and, without ceremony, the shorter one kicked me hard in the shins. I gave a shout of anguish and the door opened and four policemen in plain clothes entered hurriedly. While I hopped yelling around the room, and finally collapsed into a chair rubbing my brutalised shin, there was a short scuffle, some clicking of handcuffs and then the two champion kickers were bustled out to the waiting police car.

'Sorry about that, Eddie,' said a familiar voice and I looked up to see Pelham's large face looming over me. 'We felt we should let them get one strike in. Looks better in court.'

'Well, you're welcome to the bruise as evidence. Listen, did you get it? On tape? What he said? That should help put Cranston away. And that one with the moustache. That was him. The driver of the orange Mini. I'll testify to it in court.'

'We got it, Eddie. We got it all.'

'Marvellous,' I enthused. 'Well, I must congratulate you, Albert, on a very smooth operation. Who was in charge of it?'

'I was, Eddie.'

'You were!' I gasped, and a realisation of how close I'd been to catastrophe made me dizzy. My life, or at the very least my limbs, had been dependent on the judgement, planning and overall brain power of Albert Pelham, the thickest DC in Bristol. 'Oh, my God!'

'You needn't be upset, Eddie,' explained Pelham heavily. 'You see – I'm a sergeant now. I've been promoted.'

Chapter 9

The Superintendent turned out to be strictly a two-light-ale man. We'd got through the formalities. I'd made my statement. The goons had refused to answer any questions, as was their right, and been locked up. And by then it was opening time. I'd suggested a quick one and, to my surprise, Superintendent Bowen had agreed.

We spent a very pleasant half-hour together in the saloon bar of The Salmon and cordiality flowed. The Super was pleased because at last he really had something on Cranston. I congratulated him on the smoothness of the police operation and allowed myself to express discreet surprise at Pelham's promotion. The Superintendent astonished me by affirming that Pelham had had a very successful year. He'd passed his exams and fully deserved his promotion. I felt a slight stab of guilt. It seemed possible that if it ever came out that Pelham had accepted a beery bribe to feed me tips he might be back on the beat again or even worse. Then we discussed the murder investigation. We both agreed that it was highly unlikely that Cranston's two heavies had been responsible for the death of Maria Calderes. Not their style and no motive. And after that, we both got rather cagey. Neither of us wanted to give anything away. And then the Superintendent looked at his watch and said he had to get home because he had a guest for dinner. And I looked at my watch, and thought of the horrible mess back at the house waiting to be tidied up, and urged the Superintendent to have another. And he said:

'Two light ales. That's my lot. I made a vow when I was a DC that I wouldn't drink heavily. And I don't. I've seen too many coppers drink away their careers. Can I get you one before I go?'

I shook my head.

'No, I want to call in at the station. Might have been some interesting phone-ins after my broadcast.' Then I couldn't resist fishing for a compliment. 'How'd it strike you?'

'Excellent.'

'Really?'

'Oh yes. By the end I found I was riveted to my seat, gripping the arms of my chair with whitened knuckles.'

'Well, that's certainly ——' And I realised I'd been had. I nodded ruefully. 'Read a lot of thrillers, do you, Superintendent?'

He shook his head.

'No, but I write them occasionally. I've even had one published. It was called *Murder on the Trout Stream*. The killer used a poisoned fly. The book sold eight hundred copies.'

'Congratulations. I used to write thrillers but I never managed to get any published. I don't suppose eight hundred copies brought in much in the way of royalties, did it?'

'No, not much. About enough to buy ten cases of Guinness.'

And he rose, nodded with a smile, and departed. I gazed after him, stunned. Ten cases of Guinness? Then he knew. Albert! Christ, had I ruined his career? Or could it be just coincidence? But *ten* cases of Guinness? I rose hurriedly and followed the Superintendent. He was just getting into his car when I caught up with him. What could I say? I wanted to find out what he knew.

'Erm – just one more thing, Superintendent. Am I still a suspect?'

'Well, you are officially, Mr Shoestring. But I fancy Dixon myself.'

I swallowed and repeated stupidly:

'Dixon? Did you say Dixon?'

'Yes, you know. One of the outsiders I showed you a picture of. You asked Pelham to get you details about him.'

'What? Now, just a minute, Superintendent ——'

He was smiling at me in a slightly mocking way. And then I caught on.

'Of course! Albert's been watching me – for you. The bastard's a double agent.'

'We have to keep an eye on the competition, Mr Shoestring.'

'Ten cases of Guinness,' I said bitterly.

'Officially, of course, it should go into the police pound. But Albert's been working very hard recently and I felt he deserved a little bonus. And, as you know, he *is* fond of a drop of Guinness.'

I sighed to signify defeat. I asked:

'And why are you telling me?'

'Albert's being transferred, now that he's a sergeant. So he won't be available as a go-between any longer. If you want any more information, Mr Shoestring, apply to me direct.'

'Thanks,' I said, with as much irony as I could muster.

The Superintendent got into his car and drove off. I walked to mine and did likewise. Dixon? Good. Let the Superintendent busy himself with a false lead. I had a big ace up my sleeve. I knew a whole side of the case he didn't even suspect. Should I go to the station? No, Don could sort the calls. He'd give me a bell if there was anything I should know. And tomorrow I hoped I'd be on the track of the murderer. If what I thought – if what I was almost certain of – was right, it would take a lot of leg-work and telephoning but it would be just routine. Within a day or two, I should be face to face with him.

I stopped at a supermarket and bought a frozen pizza and a bottle of plonk. I drove home and surveyed the ruined living room with a heavy heart. I started clearing up the mess. After a while, I knocked off, went into the kitchen, thawed out my pizza and grilled it. It tasted rather like rubber with a coating of glue on top. I washed it down with half the bottle of plonk, which tasted something like stagnant water in which a few dead dogs had been floating. I swore

155

a great oath never again to eat pizza or drink wine from a supermarket. I went upstairs to the bathroom and cleaned my teeth but this process failed to remove all trace of the flavour or even of the pizza which seemed to have set like cement between my teeth. As I was cleaning my teeth, a horrid thought struck me. Had the heavies turned over my room before starting on the living room? I rushed upstairs. Thank God. I'd intruded on their wrecking before they'd got very far. My room was untouched. I opened a drawer to make sure its contents were undisturbed and found myself gazing at a full half-bottle of whisky. Odd. I had no recollection of placing it there. The taste of the pizza was still polluting my mouth. I sat down thoughtfully on the bed and uncapped the whisky. An hour later, I keeled over sideways and slept like a log.

I was awakened by a horrid squealing. What was it? Cats making love? I opened my eyes. It was still dark. I listened. The squealing rose in intensity. Tigers making love? And, as far as I could judge, downstairs in the living room. Very inconsiderate, I muttered to myself. A hard-working private eye needs his rest. If tigers are desperate for a place to consummate their illicit affair they should go to one of those hotels that cater for such things. But what was this? The tigers were being very articulate. They were squealing things like: 'Bloody hell!' 'My God!' 'Oh no!' Couldn't be tigers. Curious and resentful, I heaved myself off my bed and crept downstairs. The sounds had stopped. The light in the hall was on. I stole to the door of the living room. Erica was seated on the slashed sofa, crying softly.

'Erica!' I exclaimed, trying to fill my voice with joyous enthusiasm. 'Welcome home.'

She reached down for a broken flower vase and hurled it at me. The jagged edge might have caused a very nasty gash if it had connected. She buried her face in her hands and resumed sobbing. I went and stood over her. I cleared my throat.

'You must be tired and hungry,' I ventured. 'Can I make you something to eat? Some nice rice pudding or ——'

'I hate you!' she said. 'I'm not just saying it as girls do in novels. I hate your guts, Eddie Shoestring.'

'You're upset because of the mess,' I urged sympathetically.

She removed her head from her hands. She sniffed firmly. She stood up. She did not look at me. Instead she walked over to the fireplace and stood facing it. She said:

'I am upset because of the mess. I find it very upsetting. I think it's upsetting to fly halfway round the world to the hottest hell on earth to do a favour for your lodger and come back to find that he's destroyed your home. The mess upsets me quite a bit. And the worst bit of it is the two-legged mess. So kindly go upstairs and assemble your belongings and leave this house for ever. Get out of my life, Shoestring.'

'All right, Erica,' I said humbly. 'If that's what you want, that's what I'll do. But I want you to know that I'm not responsible for this mess. It was two men looking for a book.'

'Avid readers, were they? Get out, Shoestring.'

'Erica, I was nearly beaten to death in this room.'

'Don't torment me with might-have-beens.'

'Erica,' and I was conscious of a faint start of relief. She was cross, furious, hopping mad but she wasn't really going to send me packing. 'As a result of what happened in this room, two savage men are in police custody and the world is a safer place.'

'Not my world. My world is destroyed.'

And her shoulders heaved. She was sobbing again. I hastened to her and put my arm round her shoulder. She shrugged it off but not too fiercely. I said mournfully:

'It's awful, darling. Terrible. I know how much your things meant to you. I'd have given anything – anything at all – if I could have saved them for you. But there is a silver lining. The station will pay for everything. You'll be able to restock completely at the expense of Radio West. I know the new things won't have the same sentimental value as the old but you could buy some really nice pieces – even better than the old ones.'

She raised a moist face towards me.

'Honestly? I'll get compensation?'

'Compensation? When Don congratulated me earlier he gave me carte blanche. He was horrified at the damage. He wants you to buy anything – the sky's the limit – anything you need and a bit extra because – well, the fact is that what I did today is worth it to the station.'

'What did you do today? Apart from inviting thugs in to wreck my home?'

'Let's go into the kitchen. I'll tell you about it while I make you something.'

'I don't want something. I ate on the plane and again on the train. But I wouldn't mind a drink. Have you got any whisky?'

'No, no whisky. But there's a half-bottle of rather good red wine we can share. Are you sure you wouldn't like some rice pudding?'

'Why the hell would I want any rice pudding? I've been living on rice for the past week.'

'Of course. Well, come on – we'll go into the kitchen and drink the wine and I'll give you the whole story.'

But I didn't complete it. About halfway through Erica blinked at me owlishly, shook her head giddily and said:

'Oh God, I think it's jet lag or something. I want bed.'

I escorted her up to her bedroom and tucked her in. Then I returned to the living-room and spent a good hour and a half working on it. I didn't want her to wake in the morning and be confronted by the sordid scene again. Of course, the real damage couldn't be mended that easily and naturally I had no reason to think that Don really would stump up the pretty penny it would cost to replace the ruined furniture. But we'd cross that bridge when we came to it. At about five in the morning, I went upstairs and got into bed with Erica. And at about seven in the morning, still asleep as far as I could judge, she put her arms round my neck and hugged me close to her warm, silky, heavenly body. And at half-past nine, her teasmade, which I'd had the foresight to set, whistled and, friends once more, we sat up in bed and drank tea.

'Now, shall I continue?' I asked.

'About the arrests? No. Not yet – what I want to know is – what was the clue?'

'What clue?'

'Oh, Eddie! When I phoned you – from Manila. You sounded as if you'd had a revelation.'

'So I had.'

'Well, what was it? It didn't seem to me that I'd come up with anything much.'

'Did you check up on the other thing? Like I asked?'

'Yes.'

'And?'

'And you were right. They've got a boy.'

'About eight years old, half-European and called Johnny?'

'Yes. How did you know?'

'And Maria Calderes' child – that died in infancy? You saw the death certificate?'

'Yes, they showed it to me:'

'Did they seem very upset about it?'

'Well – not really. It was hard to tell – using an interpreter. But – what are you getting at?'

'Three boys. Three boys – and there should only be two.'

'Why should there only be two? I don't understand.'

'You will. Listen, we'll have a light breakfast because we're going to have a substantial lunch at a hotel.'

'Will you explain to me?'

'I'll do better than that. I'll take you with me and you can watch for yourself the last act of the drama unfolding.'

Over breakfast, I finished off the story about Cranston's two heavies and the Mantis manuscript. Then I told her about Jean Cole and my encounter with her American suitor. And then it was time to set off for the hotel where I hoped the final piece of the jigsaw would fall into place.

When we got to the hotel, I asked for the powerful little American by the name he'd given me: Edgar Timson, and soon he joined us in the lobby. I introduced Erica as my secretary and then he said:

'I've arranged for us to have lunch in my suite. I guess

you'd rather this was a private session, wouldn't you, Shoestring?'

'Yes. Don't want any eavesdropping. What about the boy?'

'He's gone to the movies with some people we met here in the hotel. Figured he should be out of the way, too.'

I nodded. We went upstairs to the comfortable quarters of the Mississippi brothel-keeper. Jean Cole was there, looking haggard. I tried to reassure her.

'Don't worry,' I said. 'I have an idea it's all going to come out right – for you, anyway.'

'For Maria,' she said glumly, 'it has not come out all right.'

'And we both want to catch her murderer, don't we?'

Jean nodded.

We sat down to lunch. I toyed with my sea-food cocktail and then began.

'Okay,' I said. 'I'm going to do it the way they do it in detective stories. I'm going to tell you it the way I think it was. You correct me when I go wrong – and add anything you think might be helpful. Okay?'

'Go ahead, Mr Shoestring,' said Timson courteously.

I began.

'Maria Calderes contacted me and asked me to marry her. She said she wanted British nationality so that she could bring her child over here. I saw her twice. Then she was murdered and the police suspected that I might be the murderer. I started investigating and found some odd things. Maria Calderes didn't have a child. Her child had died in infancy. Unless she'd had another child since and there was no evidence for that. Then again she'd said the Home Office was trying to deport her and they denied it. That's when I came to see you, Mrs Cole, and saw your child, Johnny – you remember?'

She nodded.

'There was something Maria had said to me which held the clue. But what was it? I couldn't bring it to mind. The police took away my passport and Erica here kindly agreed to go to the Philippines for me and do some investigating. I had an idea she'd find something – some little thing – which would put me on the right track. She did. She found out that the name of Maria Calderes' dead child was Johnny – just like yours, Mrs Cole. Odd, isn't it?'

'I think you know the reason.'

'I think I do. But let me go on in my own way. As soon as Erica told me that, on the telephone from Manila, I knew what it was that Maria had said to me in the car which was so important. She'd said: "I want to make a proper home for my child." Not a home but a *proper* home. What could that mean? Her child was supposed to be in the Philippines. It was supposed, according to her story, to be with her parents. That would be a proper home. The only thing it could have meant was that her child had a home but not a real, family home – not a home with its blood relations. That home was with you, wasn't it, Mrs Cole? Your Johnny isn't really your Johnny at all, is he? He's Maria Calderes' child.'

She sighed and said: 'I looked after him. I was good to him.'

'I know that,' I agreed. 'I know that because I know what Maria Calderes was like. She would never have allowed her child to be unhappy. But it still wasn't a *proper* home, was it?'

'No.'

'Now this is what I think happened. Maria Calderes had a child in the Philippines. She and her family were poor. She had to come over here to work so that she could send money back to support it. She met you here, Mrs Cole ——'

'You can call me Jean.'

'All right, Jean. You became friends. But Maria missed her child badly.'

'Very badly,' agreed Jean fervently. 'At nights, she would cry and cry. She would look at his picture.'

'And then – and correct me if I go wrong – and then you became pregnant, Jean. Right?'

'Right.'

'And then Maria had the idea ——'

'No,' said Jean firmly. 'It was not then. What happened, I wanted to get rid of my child. And Maria was not pleased.'

That lunch lasted nearly three hours. So I'd better tell you the essence of the story, most of which I'd already worked out, in my own words.

Maria tried to talk Jean out of having an abortion. She was a practising Catholic and, although she had an illegitimate baby herself, she was shocked by the idea. But Jean was determined. She was still young and she liked men and she didn't want to be lumbered with a baby – particularly on her small wage. Then again she hoped to be married herself one day and an illegitimate child would be no help towards that. Then Maria suggested that Jean send the baby back to the Philippines to be looked after by Jean's parents as Maria's baby was looked after by her parents. But Jean pointed out that, although her family was not as poor as Maria's, they would nevertheless expect her to contribute lavishly towards its bringing up. Jean didn't want to part with what little she had. Then Maria said that she would help support it. Jean asked how she could possibly manage that on her income? Maria said that she intended to study hard and finally get a good job. But Jean still refused. She didn't want to burden her friend. And it was only then, after the discussion had been going on for weeks and while Jean was still trying to find an abortionist, that Maria had her great idea. Jean would have the baby and she would marry its father, thus giving the baby British nationality. Then she would go home to the Philippines for a holiday, hand the baby to her parents and return with Maria's baby. A babe in arms is a babe in arms and the authorities would never notice the switch, especially as both infants were half-English. Maria was ecstatic at the thought of being reunited with her baby. But Jean thought the scheme was crazy. The father, a lay-about called Bill Cole, would never marry her and Maria would have to send money home to the Philippines to support Jean's baby and – it was quite impossible. But, at the thought of having her baby with her, Maria swept all obstacles aside. She had saved up some money. They would

162

use it to bribe Cole. She would get a very good job and send money back to the Philippines. And what about supporting her own baby over here, asked Jean. Maria had thought of that too. Jean would get a little flat and have the baby with her. Maria would pay for it, or contribute towards it, and would be able to visit frequently. But it would cost a fortune, Jean protested. Never mind, said Maria, she would be responsible for the money. The upshot was that the scheme was put into operation and, crazy though it seemed, it worked.

Cole married Jean. Jean called her baby, when it was born, Johnny, like Maria's baby, to facilitate the switch. She went back to the Philippines and exchanged the two children. And Maria studied and studied and finally ended up as manageress of Buttercups, earning quite good money. Maria remained desperately poor because she had to support Jean's baby in the Philippines and her own baby and Jean, in Bristol. In spite of that, she was happy. She had her Johnny with her. Jean was a good guardian, a little lax in morals and sometimes they had quarrels because Maria knew that Jean went with men for money and worried about its effect on Johnny, but Jean was kind and cheerful. The boy was happy. And, for safety's sake, he grew up thinking that Jean was his mother and Maria his aunt.

This situation lasted for some four years, until Johnny was about eight. Then Jean met Edgar Timson and, before long, he asked her to marry him and go to live in America. He was prepared to take Johnny too. At that time, he still thought the boy was Jean's child. Now, he knew the whole story.

Jean told Maria about the proposal. Maria was panic-stricken. She couldn't bear the thought of losing Johnny again. But he was in the country illegally. She didn't dare tell the Home Office about it. She offered Jean more money to stay but Jean wanted to be married and wanted to see America. The situation dragged on for a few weeks. Timson returned to Mississippi, giving Jean a final date for her decision. When it got near, Jean told Maria that she was sorry but she was going to accept the offer. She would have to take the child back to the Filipines and give it to Maria's parents and then go on to the USA. At about this stage, Maria came to see me with her offer. According to her thinking, she had to lie to me. And the simplest and most convincing lie she could think of was to say that she was in the situation of a lot of Filipino girls and was about to be deported. I told her I couldn't marry her. The next time I met her, she mentioned that she had accidentally bumped into the father of her child and was on her way to see him. Three days later she was found strangled in a wood near Buttercups.

When we had reached this stage, I asked Jean: 'Did Maria say anything to you about having met the father?'

'No.'

'Did you know him? This father?'

'No. It happened in the Philippines and I did not know Maria there. But she talked about him. I never understood how it happened because Maria was a good girl. I am sure she was a virgin. She was very young. I know she did not know him long. So why should a girl like that – a Catholic – get pregnant? I never understood and she did not say a lot. But I know that he was English and that he was an actor.'

I swallowed. I felt my heart beating in nervous anticipation. This was the big question.

'Jean, did Maria ever mention his name?'

'Oh yes – many times. Not his last name. But he was called Chris.'

In the car, on the way home, Erica said:

'But what about the death certificate, which I saw?'

'It's a minor industry in Manila – phoney certificates. For a very reasonable twenty quid, you can be a Fellow of the Royal College of Surgeons.'

'So what's the scenario? Maria bumped into, just by chance, this actor, this Chris. We don't know what happened but we can assume it wasn't a particularly blissful reunion. Then Jean told her she wanted to go to America. Maria had to acquire British nationality so that she could pretend to bring Johnny over here and it would be legal.

She first went to this art dealer that she'd had an affair with. He turned her down. She then tried the same proposal with you and you turned her down. Finally, in desperation, she went back to the Manila Chris – and he murdered her. Why?'

'I intend to ask *him* that.'

'But you must have a theory?'

'I have no theory. I can think of a dozen possibilities but no theory. All I know is that this whole investigation has been pointing towards him.'

'How will you find him?'

'Voice-work and leg-work, the two trusty standbys of the private eye.'

But it took a lot of leg-work and a lot of voice-work and then, three days later, Erica came home from work and invited me to join her in a pizza and a glass of wine.

'Supermarket pizza?' I asked suspiciously.

'No, super pizza. I'm going to make it myself from this pizza kit from the supermarket.'

'Keep it for the next time you get a flat tyre. Erica, you poor, barbarous gastronomic illiterate, why have I wasted my time trying to educate you in some of the finest temples of haute cuisine?'

'In the hope that I'll make you Sole Normande and Chicken Kiev, but I won't. Time is too valuable to waste on cooking.'

'Well, for me, this evening, it's too valuable to waste on eating. I'm going to the theatre.'

'Nonsense, you never go to the theatre.'

'Well, I am this evening.'

'And what,' she asked sceptically, 'are you going to see?' '*Othello*.'

'*Othello? Othello*'s not on in Bristol.'

'Oh dear. Then I suppose I shall have to go all the way to London.'

'What is this?'

'This is what,' I said, and triumphantly handed her a playbill.

She read it, murmuring in wonder.

'The Folio Players – oh, I've heard of them. They're supposed to be rather good for swinging, sexy classics. The Folio Players at the Pimlico Empire for a short season. Their much-acclaimed production of *Othello* ——'

She looked up at me in bewilderment.

'So?' she asked.

'Look at the names of the company.'

She read the names out loud until she came to:

'Christopher Simmons ——' Then she looked up at me sharply. 'Is that ——?'

I handed her a photostat of an old programme and said:

'And this one goes back nearly nine years. It's from a group that was performing in a small town near Manila. Look at the cast list.'

She ran her eye down it and soon exclaimed:

'Christopher Simmons!'

'In those days he was with a company specialising in religious plays. They were touring the Philippines. Look at the part he was playing.'

She looked and asked uncomprehendingly:

'John the Baptist?' Then she caught on. 'Johnny!'

'Right. There are two half-Filipino boys to commemorate his triumph in that part. And one dead girl. Well, I must dash. Don't want to miss the curtain.'

But the train was late and the taxis were all taken and I not only missed the curtain but half the first act. They didn't want to let me in until the act ended, but I told them I was a Shakespeare addict from Bristol who might resort to a bare bodkin if denied my fix and finally, with much reproach, I was allowed to stand at the back until the act ended. Ignoring their admonition, I asked the programme girl in a whisper:

'Which is Christopher Simmons?'

And she replied crossly: 'Shhh!' But then she relented and added 'Othello'. And I watched the man who, I was certain, had murdered an Oriental girl, make love to a white girl while decked out with a black face.

And now I have to make an admission which will probably shock and horrify most of you readers. I didn't know the play *Othello*. I had never read it or seen it performed. Naturally, all you cultured people who can quote most of Shakespeare by heart will be utterly disgusted and I wouldn't make the admission at all except that it has a bearing on my story.

Anyway, lacking any previous acquaintance with *Othello*, I found myself gradually getting hooked as the great tragedy unfolded. I tried to concentrate on studying Simmons but the play kept appropriating more and more of my attention. The only thing that marred my absorption in it was Simmons himself. Now I'm no great judge of dramatic form but it struck me he wasn't really up to the mark. I could feel that it was a titanic part with this great, noble but fairly simple-minded black general progressively ensnared in the evil net of the foul, racist Iago. The company as a whole seemed to me excellent but Simmons let the side down. He had a rather high-pitched voice without enough resonance or volume and he didn't speak the lines with ease or conviction. In spite of this, when scene two, the fatal scene, of the last act began with Othello's terrible attempt to shift the guilt of his murderous intention on to an abstract principle of morality by saying: 'It is the cause, it is the cause, my soul . . .' I literally felt prickles running down my spine. It was going to happen, before my eyes, a hideous inversion of what had happened earlier in reality. Then, this Christopher Simmons, with his own white face, had placed his hands around the neck of an Oriental girl and strangled the life out of her. Now, on the stage before me, Christopher Simmons, pretending to be a Moor, was placing his hands around the throat of a white girl and choking her to death. I almost jumped up and shouted: 'Stop!' But I held my seat and watched the murder and then Othello's downfall, marvelling at how Simmons, with his real deed heavy on his conscience, could utter the terrible plea for expiation:

'Whip me, you devils,
From the possession of this heavenly sight.
Blow me about in winds, roast me in sulphur,
Wash me in steep-down gulfs of liquid fire!
O Desdemona, Desdemona dead . . .'

There wasn't a great deal of applause when the final curtain fell, largely, I suspected, because of Simmons' mediocre performance but I found myself clapping hard. It was for the play. I wanted to rush straight off and pore over a copy, getting the boom of those lines again. But I had a 'cause' of my own that wouldn't keep.

I left the theatre with the rest of the audience and went round to the alley beside it where, as I'd suspected, the stage door was located. The push-levered metal doors were ajar and through them I could see the stage doorman, reading a newspaper in his little box. I took a deep breath, pulled open the doors and charged in, straight up to the doorman.

'Great!' I exclaimed. 'Wasn't he great? Wasn't Chris great?'

The doorman eyed me sourly.

''Aven't seen the performance myself,' he grunted.

'It's amazing. At drama school, he was – well, he wasn't supposed to be the new Olivier. But after this he could do anything. Anything! Where's his dressing-room? I've got to tell him.'

'Your name, please, sir?'

'No, no, no – I want to surprise him. I haven't seen him since we were at RADA together. But he was my best friend there. He must have talked about me? Paul Tapley?'

'Well, I don't know about ——'

'Do you watch the box? Have you seen the comedy series *A Life of Crime*? Well, I'm Boxer, the Liverpool pickpocket. You can have my autograph if you want.'

'Well, I don't mind, but ——'

'I'll give it you on my way out. But which is Chris's dressing room? Quick, man, before my enthusiasm goes off the boil.'

He shook his head faintly and then said: 'Number one, just down the passage.'

I charged off in the direction he'd indicated and then charged back again.

'By the way,' I said. 'There's a policeman sniffing around that van parked on the double yellow. Is it yours? The black Bedford?'

He shook his head.

'No, our costume van's in dock. Anyway, it's blue – dark blue.'

'Just thought I'd mention it – save you a ticket. Right, now where's that great – actor!'

And I charged once more along the corridor, until I'd turned a corner. Then I slowed down and walked more sedately to dressing-room number one. I paused a moment. Then I reached down, turned the handle and strode in.

Chapter 10

He was sitting staring at himself in the big mirror of his dressing-table. It was hard to tell for sure because he was still in his black make-up and wearing what I assumed was an artificial beard, but I thought he looked drawn and tense. Well, he had a lot to be drawn and tense about. I saw the eyes in the reflection in the mirror flick over and he frowned. He turned round to look at me and said:

'Well?'

'I just saw your performance,' I said.

'Great, wasn't it?' he said in a neutral voice that seemed as if it might just contain a hint of self-mockery.

'It certainly was for me. I've never seen *Othello* before.'

He frowned irritably.

'I don't know you. Do I? Do I know you?'

'No, you don't. But you might know my name. It's Shoestring – Eddie Shoestring.'

'Very picturesque. Why should I know it?'

'I'm a private investigator – a detective.'

He swallowed.

'I see. Are you here in a professional capacity?'

'I am, yes. And in this case it coincides with a personal capacity. You see, the police think I'm a murderer. They think I did what you just pretended to do. They think I strangled a girl to death.'

He blinked a few times and shook his head nervously.

'I don't understand – what girl? What's it got to do with me?'

'Well, it would help my case if I could demonstrate to the police that I didn't strangle her to death but that someone else did. You, for example.'

He jumped to his feet. He was a fair-sized man but I felt I could handle him. I didn't want to since I've always had a distaste for the rough side of my calling but I felt I could. He shouted: 'Get out! Get out of my dressing-room!'

At this point, the door opened and a prematurely balding young man entered saying:

'Super, Chris, but I think we should go over – oh, you've got someone with you. I'll come back later.'

And he left as swiftly as he'd arrived. As soon as we were alone again, I said firmly:

'The murdered girl was called Maria Calderes.'

It went home. He stared at me for a moment with a face like a mask. Then it sort of wrinkled up and he sat down again and covered his face with his hands. A moment later, I realised that he was crying. I approached him.

'Do you want to tell me about it?' I asked gently.

He looked up. Tears were streaming down his face, causing furrows in his make-up where white shone through.

'Murdered?' he asked helplessly. 'Maria's been murdered?'

I nodded and said, 'She was strangled to death.'

'And you think I murdered her? Me? Why should I do a thing like that?'

'I don't know, Mr Simmons. Why should you?'

'Of course I didn't murder her. Of course I didn't. Oh my God, how awful.'

'But you knew her, didn't you, Mr Simmons?'

'I——' he looked as if he might be about to deny it. But then he nodded. 'Yes, I knew her.'

'When did you last see her?'

'Nine years ago – in Maratapi.'

'And you haven't seen her since?'

'No. No, I haven't.'

'And yet – after nine years – you immediately recognised her name?'

'Well, of course I did. Because I'm constantly thinking of her – always – what I did to her——'

'What did you do to her?'

'I ——' He gazed straight past me for a long time, without moving, without, as far as I could see, even blinking and then, still very rigid, he said: 'All right, I'll tell you. I'll tell you exactly if you really want to know. I've never told anyone else but I'll tell you. It's not very pretty. It's made me the rotten person I am. I think it's probably destroyed me as an actor, too. Because actors are supposed to love themselves and I've been unable to do that – because of Maria. But I'll tell you if you want to know.'

'I'd like to know, Mr Simmons.'

'I was a Catholic in those days,' he said abruptly. Then he smiled faintly. 'I was a good Catholic, too, and worked hard to keep myself in a state of Grace. I wanted to use my – great talent in the service of God. So I got a job with the Gospel Players. I was the star of that company, which will give you some idea of the standard. But I was better then. They let me play any part I wanted. We did bible plays. In India and Africa I played Jesus Christ. Wonderful, playing God. Then when we got to the Philippines, I felt I wanted a change and so I played John the Baptist and it was very refreshing. In some ways it was a more rewarding part than Jesus who has to be meek and mild much of the time whereas John the Baptist can stride about and flash fire from eye and lips. I know I was good because one day, or rather night, in Maratapi, a very pretty Filipino girl came to my dressing-room to ask for my autograph. She'd been totally knocked out by my performance. She was a good Catholic and I was a good Catholic but the problem was that she was so bloody pretty. I let her hero-worship me and while she did so my thoughts got more and more secular. She had that irresistible combination of innocence and voluptuousness. I tried to stop thinking about sex and how easy it would be with a girl like this – who seemed to think I might actually be John the Baptist. Well, we were together, in my dressing-room, having a little drink of whisky now and then from my supply, for hours. And at the end of it we decided to get married because we both had such a burning faith and felt just the same about the church and every other blessed thing. And once we'd decided to get married, it was just as if we were married already and it seemed totally natural for me to kiss my bride in Christ. And so that's what I did. And after we'd kissed for a while we neither of us could see any particular reason, since we were already one in the eyes of the Lord, why we shouldn't consummate our spiritual marriage. So that's what we did – four times. She turned out to be a virgin but giving herself to me – to John the Baptist – was more like becoming a nun than a harlot. At least, so I managed to convince her. And then finally she left because her parents were very strict with her and had only allowed her to go to the theatre because it was a religious play. We arranged that she'd come back the following day at noon and we'd just – yes, without any fuss – go and get married. It would be a civil wedding, of course. The church wedding could follow and then she'd come back to England with me and we'd lead a blissful, Godly life and have Godly children. And that was really what I intended when I kissed her goodnight. Only ——'

He paused and gazed hard at the wall. I prompted him: 'Only?'

'Well, the usual, you know. I got cold feet. I couldn't – when I really came to think about it – see much future for the marriage. I didn't really want to get married, especially to an Oriental girl. And, after all, it would be hard on her in London. She'd have to adapt to a quite different life-style. No, she'd certainly be very miserable in London. The climate alone would depress her. No, it had been beautiful but it was clearly out of the question, just not on. And the upshot was that I went to the company manager and told him that I'd had a telegram to say that my mother was dying and I took the next plane back to England. And, of course, for a long time I wondered if there'd be any sequel if her enraged family would ambush me one day in West Hampstead or if I'd have an official letter from some government department or a lawyer or – but there never was anything. I left religious theatre and went in for the classical theatre and every bloody day since then I've remembered what I did to Maria Calderes.'

'And that's all you did to her? Seduce her?'

'Isn't it enough?'

'And what about when you bumped into her?'

His eyes narrowed.

'How do you mean?'

'When you bumped into her a few months ago – here in England?'

He shook his head positively.

'I haven't seen her since I flew out of Manila nine years ago.'

'She said that you bumped into her.'

'Then she was lying.'

I sighed.

'There seems to be a lot of lying in this case. Where were you ——?'

And I gave the date on which Maria Calderes had been murdered.

'Where was I? I was in ——' He turned through a little engagements book on his desk. 'Yes, of course. I was in Manchester. We were touring *Othello*.'

Manchester? If that was true, he was in the clear. There was no way he could have been performing in *Othello* in Manchester and murdering Maria Calderes in London on the same evening. The police time of death was firm.

'Can you prove that?' I asked.

'Of course I can prove it. Ask the director, ask anyone in the company. We were in Manchester, doing *Othello*.'

I nodded.

'All right,' I said. 'I will. But the police will doubtless want a statement from you.'

'The police? But – why must you tell the police? I can prove I was in Manchester.'

'I told you. I'm a suspect and that means I have to keep in with the Old Bill. I can't withhold evidence.'

'But it's not evidence. Not if I ——'

'Was in Manchester. Right. But they'll still be interested. If your alibi holds, you've got nothing to worry about, have

174

you? Can you drive, Mr Simmons?'

'Drive? What, a car?'

'Not a herd of cows. Do you have a driving licence?'

'Certainly. Why?'

'Just wondered. I'll be going but I'm not saying I won't be returning. And I think you'll see the police before long.'

He shrugged wearily.

'I'm guilty all right but not of anything criminal. Goodbye, Mr ——'

'Shoestring.'

'Goodbye.'

I went in and checked with the director who'd looked in earlier. He confirmed Simmons' story. He even showed me posters from the Manchester run. It seemed that Christopher Simmons could not have murdered Maria Calderes.

I left the theatre.

I felt dispirited. More than that, I felt frightened. Who had killed Maria Calderes? There were two suspects, both called Christopher and both admitting to having seduced her. If it wasn't Christopher Simmons then presumably it must have been Christopher Dixon. But I couldn't make myself believe that. He'd had no motive. Even supposing he was a professional hit-man, the one thing such people avoid is senseless killing. The more jobs you do the more your chances of getting caught. And Dixon, in the unlikely event that he was the man the police were looking for in connection with the murder of criminals in various parts of England, was a professional who shot people with a silenced automatic. Why would he suddenly strangle an innocent girl to death? But if neither Dixon nor Simmons had killed her then it must have been someone else. And the only someone else in the police dossier at the moment was Eddie Shoestring. I hadn't, until this point, really taken seriously the possibility of finding myself on trial for murder. But I knew the law wasn't infallible. Innocent men had, in the old days, gone to the gallows and there was good reason to think that several men were, at the present time, serving sentences for murders they had never committed. I suddenly saw a cell stark and clear. I'd been in cells, as a visitor, a number of times. They're not pleasant. They're big enough to pace five paces in one direction and none in the other direction and a small patch of daylight reaches you through a grid of three separate layers of bars. The most frightening thing is the door with its concave peep-hole. It's made of thick, impervious steel against which, in the case of a fire, say, a man could beat himself desperately with no more hope of escape than a canary from a cage. The walls are bare brick and the floor is bare concrete and altogether such a place would not constitute a desirable residence for Shoestring for the next fifteen years.

I shuddered and looked about for a pub but when I found one it was closed. I looked at my watch. Quarter to twelve. Would I make the last train? Why bother? If I was really heading for Pentonville or Parkhurst, I'd have one more sumptuous night before the grating keys and clanging gates began. I went back to the hotel on Miramar Street and, of course, they didn't have a room. An hour later I found a vacancy in a hotel which had rooms so tiny and airless they made me think of cells. And that was the last thing I wanted to think of. So I phoned down to room service, which turned out to be an old man with one arm, for a bottle of whisky. Naturally he hadn't got any but he brought up a bottle of arrack. Maybe the hotel specialised in that neglected section of the floating population, poor Arabs. Anyway, I drank half the arrack which I was not used to and which first made me sick and then gave me nightmares about prison cells. One of Shoestring's worst nights ever.

In the morning, after paying the bill and a monstrous surcharge for the arrack, I left the hotel, colliding in the doorway with what was clearly a poor Arab because, even at that early hour, he reeked of arrack. I was nearly sick again on the spot. But I waved feebly at a passing taxi and, to my astonishment, it swerved to the kerb and halted. Usually they pick up speed and hurtle past with the driver grinning triumphantly at you.

'Paddington,' I muttered, climbed in and slumped.

I slept most of the way in the train, an uneasy sleep full of menace and pursuit. Sometimes I was doing the pursuing and sometimes I was the pursued. Policemen were after me, and poor Arabs and civilians with elaborate guns. Then I was in a woodland trying to find a road before I stumbled on something I didn't want to see. I heard cars passing in the distance but I knew that each step I was taking was leading me closer to a clearing where – and the train stopped and I awoke.

There were things to be done but I had no heart to do them. And I felt dirty. That hotel had somehow been unwholesome. I wanted a wash and shave. I got my car from the multi-storey car park and drove home. I opened the door and stepped into the hall and stopped dead. There it was, as large as life and three times as heavy: an Indian boy and a cheetah fashioned in bronze. I stared at it for several minutes and then I went through to the living room and dialled a number.

'I'd like to speak to Miss Bayliss, please.'

'Well, I'm afraid she's ——'

'It's very urgent.'

'Well – hold on a minute.'

There was a long pause and then an irritated Erica.

'Hello?'

'Erica, it's me, Eddie.'

'Well, blast you, Eddie. I'm in the middle of an important conference.'

'I'm sorry. Listen, that statue ——'

'Yes, that statue! And blast you again. They woke me up this morning delivering it. What's more, it's hideous and I don't want it in the house. Have you gone mad? It must have cost a lot.'

'Erica? Did it come in a black or dark blue short-wheel-base Bedford van?'

'Oh, nonsense. I've got to go now.'

'Wait! Erica, it's important. Really.'

'I didn't see the van. Now, I've got to ——'

'Think! Think! It's very ——'

'Look, I *can't stay now*. I'm having lunch with Stu and Jill at the Cartwheel. You can join us there at one if you want.'

She hung up.

I looked at my watch. It was half-past eleven. Oh well, it would keep until one. I'd just have a wash and shave and – the doorbell rang.

I glanced through the window and saw a police patrol car outside. Was this it? Were they going to lock me up now? Well, I wasn't ready for that yet. True, I only had one slender lead left but I was going to play the game to the end. I squared my shoulders and marched briskly to the front door and pulled it open. It didn't escape me that there were two uniformed young constables there. One of them smiled pleasantly.

'Are you Mr Eddie Shoestring?'

'Right in one.'

'Superintendent Bowen's compliments and he'd like a word with you, sir.'

'You've saved me a trip. I was just about to set off and see him. I'll follow you, shall I?'

'We'd prefer it if you came in our car, sir.'

I shrugged cheerfully.

'It'll save petrol but how do I get back?'

'I'm sure the Superintendent will arrange something, sir.'

Twenty minutes later, I was back in the Superintendent's office. At least it wasn't the interview room. But Bowen had a distinctly official air about him when he said: 'Dixon's in the clear, at least for the Calderes murder.'

'Really? I'm not surprised.'

He looked sceptical.

'Why is that, Mr Shoestring?'

'Because I'm getting close to the real killer. How have you eliminated Dixon?'

'The Met's seen him. He's got an alibi.'

'Care to confide in me?'

'I think you rate that. You've helped us quite a bit with the Buttercups matter. The alibi goes as follows: Maria Calderes reached London at about four in the afternoon and at that time Dixon was having a party – I think they call it a "vernissage" – at his art gallery. His fiancée, Lady Celia Chetwynd, the Earl of Chetwynd's daughter, was there. Incidentally, aristocratic alibis are always the best. Somehow, although we live in a democracy where justice is dispensed without fear or favour, judges and juries still seem to think a title speaks the truth. Anyway, once the party was over, Dixon and his lady friend spent the evening together, had dinner out and went back to Dixon's place where she spent the night with him. Lady Chetwynd was picked up at the same time as Dixon and interviewed separately. They both told the same story.'

'Why did you say that he was in the clear "at least for the Calderes murder"?'

'Because, oddly enough, I still fancy him for the pro jobs. We've got a witness to one of them in Halifax where it happened four years ago. She's an old lady, deaf and a bit gaga. Wouldn't be much use in court but she swears, from a photograph, that he's the man she saw shooting Toby White, the porn king of the North. There are a few other suggestive things, too. Nothing we could make stick – so far.'

'So who do you fancy for the Calderes murder?'

The Superintendent coughed delicately. I said heatedly:

'Oh, come off it, Bowen. You know damned well that I didn't kill her. You know me pretty well by now. I'm not a strangling man. You've got no evidence in any case.'

'Everything you say is true, Mr Shoestring. And I didn't bring you in to arrest you. But I'm under a lot of pressure to make an arrest. So, if you've got a plausible suspect in the bag, now's the time to pull him out.'

'That's just what I'm going to do. Listen, I need forty-eight hours. If I don't come up with him by then, you can start the heavy grilling.'

'I'm taking a chance, Mr Shoestring. Don't let me down.'

I went back to the house to pick up my car, feeling distinctly creepy. What had I really got? Absolutely nothing except the frail straw of the van. But suppose the bronze *had* come in a blue-black or black van? Dixon had an alibi – a solid one. Still, villains have had alibis before now and also blood on their hands. I drove to the Cartwheel.

I was late and the merry group were in the middle of lunch. I've never gone much on Stu and Jill because they are so very arty and sophisticated. They seem to think life consists of flitting from concert to art gallery and from art gallery to theatre. They also know everyone in the arts, or at least they talk as if they do. I will admit that the one time I tried to catch them out they were able to prove with photographs that they had, in fact, just come back from a Mediterranean yacht cruise with a film star, a painter and a clutch of other creative spirits. Stu was, in fact, a feature writer who wrote articles on, needless to say, arty subjects in places like the colour sups and Jill was a children's book editor for a publishing house. Erica adored them.

As I arrived at the table, I heard Jill saying:

'Larry wasn't there but then he has been so ill lately, poor darling, but I asked Glenda about it and she ——'

I forgot to mention that they are also terrible name-droppers. I had a vague idea Jill might be talking about actors but I never found out because as soon as she saw me bearing down on them, she stopped and gaped.

'Hello,' I said.

Erica glared at me.

'Where on earth have you been?' she asked.

'How do you mean?'

'You look awful.'

'Do I? Why do I?'

'I don't know why you do. Your eyes are red.'

And then I remembered. I hadn't shaved. I'd spent that foul night in that foul hotel. I fumbled at my collar. My tie was halfway down my chest. I gulped.

'Must be the arrack. Does it give you red eyes? Hi, Stu. Hi, Jill.'

'Hello, Eddie,' returned Stu jovially. Actually, Stu wasn't too bad. At least, he always seemed friendly while his stuck-up little wife invariably snubbed me. I sat down.

'We're halfway through our meal,' said Erica pointedly.

'That's okay. I'm not going to hold you up. I didn't come to eat, anyway.'

'You want to know about the van, is that it?'

'That's it. What colour was it?'

'Van?' asked Stu interestedly. 'What van?'

Erica turned to him.

'You wouldn't believe it. At half-past seven this morning – half-past seven! – these two men arrived with the most hideous – well, I don't know what to call it. A sculpture, I suppose. It was made of bronze, anyway. And it seemed to be a dwarf with a bear.'

'Oh, cut it out, Erica,' I said wearily. 'It was a very reasonable likeness of an Indian boy with a cheetah.'

I felt intense irritation. Why did she do it? Erica was the most marvellous, natural person I know – except when she was with Stu and Jill. Then she got horribly affected.

Jill tittered.

'An Indian boy with a cheetah? Doing what, darling?'

'Doing nothing, darling,' I said savagely. 'It's a valuable work of art. But that's not the point ——'

'But it is,' she cooed. 'Since when have you gone in for works of art, Eddie?'

'It doesn't matter. The point is ——' I turned to Erica. 'Have you remembered? What colour was the van?'

'I have remembered. It was yellow.'

My heart sank.

'Yellow? Are you sure it was yellow?'

'Positive.'

'Damn.'

'But, darling,' exclaimed Jill, 'this is extraordinary. Have you turned into such a fastidious aesthete that you have to have your works of art delivered in vans of a particular colour?'

'No, I haven't, darling,' I returned. 'But I was hoping it was a black or dark blue van because that's the colour van that was used to deliver the corpse of a girl to a wood just out of town. And I'm suspected of having turned her into

181

a corpse.'

'Gracious,' said Jill. 'Did you?'

But I could see that some of the phoniness had gone out of her. I shook my head.

'No. But I'd like to be able to prove it.'

I must have looked wretched. Erica put her arm on mine.

'I'm sorry, Eddie. Why don't you have a drink?'

'Why not?'

I looked round for the waiter. He was, in that traditional way of waiters, pointedly gazing in the opposite direction. I looked back. Erica, to my gratification, was looking at me solicitously.

'How was *Othello*?' she asked.

'Pretty good,' I admitted. 'Except for the Othello. He was lousy.'

'And did you get what you were looking for?'

I shook my head. There ensued an uncomfortable pause. Then Stu said, more to break the silence, I felt, than because he was really interested in my views on the theatre:

'Where did you see *Othello*, Eddie?'

'London. Pimlico.'

'Really?' He frowned thoughtfully. 'Who was doing it?'

I shook my head.

'Some company – oh, yes, they were called The Folio Players.'

'The Folio Players?' squealed Jill. 'But they're marvellous! You remember, Stu? We saw their *Othello* in Manchester when we were there with Justin and Lorraine a few weeks ago.' She turned to Erica. 'Justin is the artistic director of Midlands Television and Lorraine does rather delicious little sound poems.' She turned to me. 'But you mean to say you didn't think Bill Turkin was superb?'

'Who did he play?' I asked dully.

'Who did he play? He played Othello, of course. I mean, Bill *is* the Folio Players.'

'No, he's not,' I said. 'At least, he wasn't when ——'

And then I stopped and gazed at her intently. I suddenly found my breathing rate had increased.

'Are you quite sure,' I asked, 'that it was the *Folio* Players you saw in Manchester?'

'Of course I'm sure.'

'And – and – it wasn't Christopher Simmons playing Othello?'

Jill shook her head distastefully.

'No, it wasn't. It was Bill Turkin,' she said.

My pocket! I'd put it in my pocket and forgotten it. I reached down and groped about in the pocket. I found it. I pulled it out, the crumpled programme. I opened it and looked feverishly down the cast list. And there it was: Othello – William Turkin. I couldn't suppress it. I gave a shout: 'An understudy! Simmons was the understudy. That's why he was so terrible! I missed the opening. They'd have announced it. He was the understudy.'

'Well, never mind, darling,' said Jill soothingly. 'When Bill's back you must catch his Coriolanus. If anything, it's ——'

'Shut up!' I snarled. I shouldn't have snarled, even although I was struggling to work it out, but then I'd wanted to snarl at Jill for such a very long time and it seemed too good an opportunity to miss.

'Sod you,' she retaliated, but softly. I continued aloud.

'Simmons isn't even on the cast list. So, in Manchester he was just an understudy. And if this other fellow was on stage, Simmons would have been free, wouldn't he?'

'How do you mean?' asked Stu.

'He could have left the theatre, driven to London and – couldn't he?'

Stu shrugged.

'Understudies are supposed to hang around – in case the star breaks a leg or something. But it depends on the company to some extent. Some are more flexible than others.'

I was hardly listening.

'It fits,' I said. 'That's it. That's how it must have been.'

I pored through the programme.

'What day is it?' I asked.

'Thursday,' said Stu.

'Matinée!' I exclaimed. 'There's a matinee today!'

I looked at my watch and then jumped to my feet.

'I can make it,' I said. 'This time I'm going to nail th bastard.'

And, aware that they were now all gaping at me, I turne and rushed out of the restaurant.

Just two and a quarter hours later, I was sitting i Christopher Simmons' dressing room, waiting for the per formance to end. I'd bribed the stage doorman with a tenne to let me in. He'd also informed me that Turkin was still i hospital, recovering from an operation for a strangulate hernia. There was a speaker in the dressing-room. I turne the dial attached to it and listened to the relay from th stage of the last few scenes of *Othello*. I heard the final line the scattering of applause. A couple of minutes later, th door of the dressing-room opened and Simmons, lookin quite knocked out, tottered into the room.

He saw me, stopped and said:

'Oh, God.'

Then he continued on past me, sat down at his dressing table, reached up and carefully peeled off his beard.

'You lied to me, Mr Simmons,' I said evenly.

He turned in his chair. He looked strange with a whit patch on his chin where his beard had been and the rest c his face still covered in black make-up.

'No, I didn't,' he said.

'You told me that you played Othello in Manchester.'

'Did I? I thought I said we were doing *Othello* in Man chester, which is the truth. What does it matter, anyway?

'It matters quite a lot. If you weren't actually on stage you could have popped down to London and killed people.'

He shook his head wearily. He looked bitter, even wit his make-up on.

'You fool,' he said, 'you bloody fool.'

He turned back to his mirror, took a pad of cotton wool put some kind of grease on it and started rubbing his face The black started to come off.

'Do you see some flaw in my theory?' I asked courteously

He stopped rubbing his face and looked at me – but only in the mirror.

'I'm a coward. I didn't even have the guts to marry the girl because she was oriental. I couldn't face my precious parents or – society – or – so where would I have found the guts to kill her?'

'Still, you could have done.'

He was rubbing his face again. The black was coming away in long swathes. He shook his head.

'No, I couldn't. I was understudying. I wasn't on stage but I was in the theatre. Ask Tim – the director – ask anyone in the company.'

'I'd like to do that.'

He reached down for the phone on his dressing-table. He dialled three digits, obviously for an internal line.

'Ricky? Could you ask Tim to step in here for a moment – and anyone else that's about? It's just a shade urgent.'

He turned round again and faced me. His face was half-clear of make-up by now. I thought there was something familiar about it but I couldn't decide what. He smiled grimly. He said:

'Kill? I don't kill things, Mr Shoestring. I don't kill spiders. I put them out of the window. I don't set mousetraps. Kill? It's such a little, simple word and perhaps in your world it's a little, simple act. But it would be easier for me to ride on a cloud than to kill a human being.'

'You do a very convincing job on Desdemona.'

'Yes, I can act killing. I do that bit rather well, don't I? But it's the only thing I do well in the whole part. I'm a wash-out as an actor. Thank God, Bill will be back next week. Do you know what I'm going to do then, Mr Shoestring? I'm going to enter a monastery as a novice. I'm going to become a monk. And if you think that testifies to a guilty conscience, you're absolutely right, but it's not because I'm a murderer——'

Just then the door opened and in came the director, a girl wearing the long skirt and wig of Desdemona, and another chap who didn't look like an actor.

'What is it, Chris?' asked the director.

Simmons waved in my direction.

'He thinks I'm a murderer. He wants to ask you some questions. Forgive me if I continue removing my make-up. It's itching badly.'

And he turned back to his dressing-table and reached for another pad of cotton wool.

Well, I asked them about the day in question and they all provided definite alibis. One of them had had coffee with Simmons, another had chatted with him and so on. While we were going through it, a couple more members of the cast entered and they too confirmed that Simmons had not left the theatre for long enough to buy a sandwich, never mind to drive to London and back. Why? I kept asking myself. Why were they all lying? Team spirit? *Esprit de corps*? Take care of your own? But I wasn't accusing this man of some trifling misdemeanour but of murder. Suddenly, I felt angry. There was a lot of chattering going on. I held up my hand for silence.

'All right,' I said. 'Listen, everyone. If I get on the phone and call Scotland Yard and they send a couple of cars full of coppers round here, are you still prepared to tell the same story? And in court, would you swear it on oath?'

There were murmurs of 'yes', 'definitely', 'why not, it's the truth' and so on.

I was furious. I took a deep breath. I was going to give them a blast of Shoestring wrath – and just then Christopher Simmons, having finished with his face, swung round to face us. I glanced at him and – all the anger went out of me. I put my hand to my head. I literally felt giddy.

'Anything wrong?' asked Tim, the director, solicitously.

I shook my head. I said:

'No, I – I've been on the go too long – bit tired, that's all.'

I approached the father of Maria Calderes' child, although I had no intention of telling him he was that, and smiled.

'Listen,' I said, 'I'm not a drama critic but when I saw you in *Othello* last night, I was really with you – all the way.

186

So you can't be a bad actor, can you?'

'I'll be a better monk.'

I shrugged.

'Your choice. But I'd like something to remember your performance by. Do you have a photograph?'

'Not in *Othello*.'

'Not important.'

He smiled ironically.

'Oh, I've got a stack of publicity stills – and I won't have much use for these any more.'

He swung back, pulled open a desk and took one out.

'Sign it for me, would you?' I asked.

At this point, Desdemona said irritably:

'Well, what about us? Are you finished with us?'

'Sorry,' I said humbly. 'Yes, thank you for your co-operation.'

There was a certain amount of muttering and they all trooped out. Simmons handed me the signed photograph. He said: 'Would you like an envelope?'

'Please.'

He handed me one and I slipped the photograph into it. He said:

'I take it you were satisfied – by my impressive list of alibis?'

'No,' I said, 'not by those. But I'm satisfied. You didn't kill Maria Calderes. And I know who did. Good luck, Mr Simmons. I think you should stay on the stage and in the world. But, of course, it's your choice.'

And I left.

I couldn't find a taxi and it took me nearly half an hour by tube and foot to reach Dixon's gallery. It was closed but I peered in and saw that the receptionist was still at her desk. I knocked and she glanced round. When she saw me, a look of irritation appeared on her face but was quickly replaced by a smile. She came and opened the door.

'Mr Shoestring,' she purred. 'Is anything wrong? As you can see, we're closed.'

I smiled apologetically.

'I know. My train's just got in. Is Mr Dixon here?'

'No, he left a good hour ago.'

'Then perhaps you could give me his address?'

'Oh, I couldn't do that. He'd be very annoyed.'

'But this is really most important. Could you phone him and ask him if he'd consent to see me?'

'I'm afraid there's no chance of that, Mr Shoestring. He never sees clients at home.'

'But I'm not here as a client. I'm here as a detective. Phone him and tell him that. I have an idea he will see me.'

She gave me a long and curious look. Then she sighed and, ushering me in, went to the telephone and dialled. After a while she said:

'Hello, Mr Dixon? I'm sorry to bother you. I have Mr Shoestring here ——'

Then she paused and listened. Then she said:

'Very well,' and hung up. She turned to me with curiosity written all over her face.

'How very odd. As soon as I gave your name, he said: "Ah, yes, I've been expecting him. Please give him my address."'

'It's perfectly simple,' I explained. 'It's an investigation that we're both concerned about.'

'Fakes? Something like that?' she asked.

'Something like that,' I agreed with a polite smile. 'Now could I have the address, please?'

She wrote it on a piece of paper and handed it to me. I thanked her and departed.

Chapter 11

'Damn it!' I shouted at the startled plump lady. 'Why don't you stock Macbeths?'

'I'm sure I don't know, sir,' she protested. 'I'm not the manager.'

'Well, call the manager.'

'He's not here now, sir. I've never heard of Macbeths.'

'They're the best cigarette ever made. They're marvellous. All these others are junk, junk, do you hear me?'

'Please don't be abusive, sir.'

'I will be abusive. I feel abusive whenever I come across stupid, unenlightened tobacconists that don't stock Macbeths. Tell the manager that, will you? Tell him Eddie Shoestring said so. Here, I'll write it down for you.'

And I pulled out my diary, tore off a sheet and wrote my name on it and the word 'Macbeths'.

'Don't forget. The next time I come in here, I want to find Macbeths on your shelves. Do you hear? That's an order! An order from Eddie Shoestring! Remember it!'

And I stalked out.

I was sorry to have upset the old dear but I wanted to leave a tracer. I wanted to make sure the police found out that I'd reached the district if I suddenly went missing. Because I knew that what I was about to do was crazy. I also knew what I should have done. And that was to phone Scotland Yard and then keep watch outside Dixon's door as the cars arrived and the blue-uniformed men stormed in. But ——

But what? Well, I had an idea that Dixon wouldn't admit anything to them. I felt that even with what I could now tell them, he might get off the hook somehow. I also had a sort of intuition that I might be the only man in England he *would* talk to. And then again – I'd said to all the fans of Radio West that I was going to bring him in myself, that I, Eddie Shoestring, was going to nail the murderer of Maria Calderes. I was crazy. I'd probably get a bullet between the eyes for my stupid vanity but I was going in alone. It would either be Shoestring's finest hour or his final one.

Ten yards from the tobacconist's, I turned into the elegant little Belgravia mews. At number seven, I rang the doorbell. A few moments later, the murderer of Maria Calderes, and of various other people, opened the door. He smiled politely.

'Hello, Mr Shoestring, do come in. We'll go upstairs to the studio, shall we? It's much the most pleasant room.'

I followed him up a short flight of stairs into a huge room that had obviously been made by knocking down dividing walls. It was full of splendid sculptures and objets d'art. I wondered in which one the silenced automatic was hidden. He said:

'That chair's particularly comfortable. Can I get you a drink?'

'Anything but arrack,' I said cheerfully, seating myself.

'Oh, is arrack in?' he asked interestedly.

'It's in me – more of it than I like. Whisky and soda would be very acceptable.'

He made one for me, even fetching ice from a small fridge under the window-seat, and prepared himself some kind of elaborate cocktail. Then he seated himself opposite me and said:

'Cheers.'

I, too, said: 'Cheers.' And we both had a sip.

'Now then ——?' he said encouragingly.

'My impression is,' I said carefully, 'that you're a kind of hobby murderer.'

He frowned thoughtfully.

'I suppose you could put it that way,' he agreed. 'It was exciting and it was a challenge. And it gave me a secret life. It's a very romantic thing to have, a secret life. Of course, I should imagine a sociologist would relate it to

190

the thing they always say about my generation. We've never had our fair share of excitement. Then the money was handy, and I felt I was doing a spot of good – shooting all those foul chaps.'

'Maria Calderes wasn't a foul chap.'

He looked distinctly thoughtful.

'No,' he agreed, 'she wasn't.'

'When I first called at your gallery – did you know who I was?'

'Oh, of course.'

I smiled in admiration.

'You gave a marvellous performance. That's what this case has been all about really: performances. It's a tale of two actors – a terrible one and a superb one.'

'He's still an actor, is he?' asked Dixon interestedly.

'Yes. Didn't you know that?'

He shook his head.

'I did think of looking him up. It even fleetingly crossed my mind that I might shoot him. But I've only ever shot villains and anyway things were getting too complicated – out of hand – by then. It's a pity really.'

'What?'

'Oh, you know – that I have this knack for acting. It wouldn't have happened otherwise.'

'You mean Maria?'

'Yes.'

I reached into the envelope that Simmons had given me and took out the photograph. I held it up in front of me and looked from it to Dixon and back. Then I handed it to him. He studied it for some time.

'It really *is* quite remarkable,' he agreed finally. 'Actually, I was hoping that he'd have changed over the years. Then, of course, it would have been hard to prove.'

I took the photograph back and looked at it again.

'You're not exactly doubles – just a strong, overall likeness. And after nine years ——'

'And the names,' he pointed out.

'But the last names are, of course, different.'

He nodded.

'I don't think she remembered his last name. Seems odd but that was the impression I had.'

'It's quite possible,' I confirmed. 'They only ever had one night of love – really only half a night. So, you booked in at Buttercups – were you after someone?'

'Yes. A drug-pusher. There was a contract out on him.'

'Did Cranston know?'

'Good Lord, no. I never worked for Cranston. My control was – well, I mustn't be indiscreet, must I?'

'And as soon as Maria saw you ——?' I deliberately left the question unfinished.

He nodded.

'She thought I was the father of her child. I suppose she checked on the register and found my name was Chris and that really convinced her. Oh, you've no idea how convinced she was.'

'So you didn't set out to seduce her?'

'No, of course not. I was there on business. Doesn't do to mix sex and work. But she came to my room that night and asked me if I knew who she was. I could see she was in a very wrought-up state. I was curious. So I said I wasn't sure. That was my fatal mistake.'

'Surely it was her fatal mistake?'

'Both of ours, I think. Anyway, I soon had the story out of her and – well, she was damned attractive.'

'So you played the long-lost Chris and had an affair with her?'

'As far as she was concerned, the resumption of an affair.'

'Weren't you worried about the complications? About the child?'

'No!'

He half-clenched his fists and a look of anger, mixed with remorse, crossed his face. He said fiercely:

'She never told me about the child! Not until it was too late. If she had – I'd have pulled out at once. I couldn't afford that kind of involvement.'

He lowered his head, closed his eyes and breathed deeply

for a moment or two. Then he raised his head and looked at me. He said with much feeling:

'Oh, Mr Shoestring, I do *wish* she'd mentioned the child.'

'When you left Buttercups, she still thought that you were Chris Simmons?'

He glanced at me.

'Simmons? Is that his name?'

I nodded.

'Well, yes, she did. I wasn't worried because – she didn't seem set on me. Rather the reverse. I realised later, of course, that it was because of the child. She was terrified to let anyone into that secret. But she did, in the end, in desperation.'

I said, 'According to Bristol CID you've got a cast-iron alibi.'

He grinned.

'It's a stage-prop, really. Looks like steel but it's just papier-mâché. We'll come to it. Well, a couple of months after that meeting, Maria came to see me in London.'

'That was true, was it?'

'Oh yes. She said the Home Office wanted to deport her. She asked me if I'd marry her just for convenience. She was quite reasonable. I was worried but not too worried. I told her that I was engaged and I couldn't. She seemed to accept it and left. And, of course, I hoped that the Home Office *would* deport her and that that would be the end of it. I still didn't know about the child. Have you seen him, incidentally?'

'Yes. He's a fine, motherless boy.'

He flinched slightly.

'Fair enough,' he said.

Cool it, Shoestring, I warned myself. No point in goading this one. I said, truthfully but also diplomatically:

'Actually, he didn't know Maria was his mother. He thought she was his aunt. As far as he's concerned his mother is still alive. But do go on.'

He smiled.

'Well, on the day that she died, she phoned me in the

morning. She sounded desperate, hysterical. She said I'd
have to marry her. She said she'd make trouble for me otherwise. She said she'd go to the Home Office, to the police.
I got a bit panicky. I told her that I'd do anything she
wanted. I asked her to come down to London and see me at
the gallery. I remembered that it was my receptionist's day
off but I'd completely forgotten that I had a vernissage that
afternoon. By the time I'd remembered and phoned her
back, she'd left.'

I asked:

'And was that when you made up your mind to kill her?'

He looked shocked.

'My God, no. I told you. I only killed swine.'

'But you did kill her?'

He nodded with a grim smile.

'Yes, in the event I did.'

'Why?'

'I wonder if I can make you understand? Actually, I find
it hard to understand myself. But I'll tell you what happened. She arrived when the vernissage was in full swing. I
suppose there were three hundred people in the gallery – the
usual thing, you know, jammed in so tight that no one could
see the pictures or much else. As it happens, there were a
dozen or so oriental girls and women in the group so that
when Maria edged her way in, she wasn't conspicuous. I
made sure no one saw us together but I beckoned her
through to my office. Then I shut the door and told her the
whole story. I told her how I'd been intrigued when she'd
first asked me: Do you know who I am? I explained how I'd
led her on to give me the background and how I'd slowly
realised that I must look very much like this other Chris, the
actor who'd seduced her. I told her how I'd then simply
exploited the information to do the same. Then I showed
her my passport which proved that I'd never been to the
Philippines. Then I apologised for what I'd done and told
her that I'd do anything reasonable to make amends. And
then I realised that she hadn't believed a word of it. She cried.
She reproached me. She said I shouldn't have gone to all the

trouble of getting a false passport just to deceive her. She said she wouldn't ask anything of me – if it wasn't for the child. What child, I asked her. And then she told me all about Johnny. And then I began to feel trapped. I'd done my work too well. In her mind, I *was* the other Chris and there seemed no way I could persuade her otherwise. I'd be stuck with her and her child for ever. I had to escape. I felt that nothing mattered but to break this identification that I'd forged myself. She must be convinced, once and for all, that I was not the man she had known in the Philippines. I began to tell her more and more about myself. I heard myself admitting – no, boasting about – things I'd told no one else in the world. Her Chris had been a Catholic. Well, I wasn't. I was an atheist. Her Chris had been a humanitarian. And I – I was a killer. Yes, I told her. I was a hired assassin and I'd shot four criminals for pay. I told her about each one in vivid detail. And I enjoyed telling her. I'd never had a chance to tell anyone before. It was exciting, almost as exciting as the deeds themselves had been. I got quite carried away. I gave her corroborative details about how I'd stayed at Buttercups at the same time as they had. I named them and specified where they'd all been killed. And then suddenly – I realised that she believed me. She was gazing at me – eyes wide in horror. I stopped talking abruptly and gazed back at her. I felt a kind of exultant despair. I'd done it – broken my cover, confessed to murder, put myself totally in the hands of this saintly, stupid Filipino girl.'

He was silent. I prompted:

'So that's why you killed her? To silence her?'

He looked at me oddly.

'I think so.'

'You think so?' I asked, astounded.

'I'm not sure. I never will be sure – now. We both knew what the situation was. It all passed between us – in the long look we exchanged. From outside the gallery came the sounds of the party. And death passed in that look. She knew now that I was a murderer. She realised that she must be the only person in the world that knew that. She wasn't surprised when I rose and moved towards her. She watched me with a kind of terrible curiosity. But while I moved towards her all kinds of things were happening in my mind. You've killed swine, I told myself, but this is different. This is a fine person. Then I thought of the Gallery and Celia and the years of high living ahead and I knew I had to silence her. Then I thought that it was impossible. I'd never be able to live with myself afterwards. And, after all, I'd always accepted the risk of being caught. The risk, in fact, had been much of the attraction, as with mountain climbers. Well, now the account had to be paid. I stood over her and I think – I think – I was going to tell her to clear out – get out – run to the police ——'

'But you didn't?' I asked, fascinated by his tale.

'No.'

'Why not?'

'As I stood over her – and I suppose she must have read her danger from my stance – she suddenly said in a thin little voice: "Don't do it, Chris. Think of our son." And I felt a spurt of rage. It had all been useless. I'd put my life – or at least my freedom – in her hands to convince her that I wasn't the man she thought I was. And she still hadn't accepted it. I'd convinced her I was a murderer all right but she still thought I was the Chris she'd known in the Philippines. So, when I put my hands to her throat and squeezed, I'm not sure if it was to silence her or because I was simply goaded beyond endurance by her stubbornness. I had to break it and this was the only way left to me.'

He was silent again and this time I didn't attempt to prompt him. He sighed deeply and said:

'She didn't struggle much. She put her hands to my wrists and tugged feebly but that was all. And I think it was because she still loved me. She thought the man who had taken her virginity and fathered her child was now taking her life and she accepted it. She died without ever realising that she'd had sexual relations with more than one man.'

There was a long silence. Then I asked:

196

'What did you do then?'

His manner became brisk.

'Oh then? Well, the pro reflexes came into play. Once it was done I thought about covering my tracks. With my contract jobs, of course, I'd always planned every detail. Now I had to improvise. But it turned out to be surprisingly easy. I had a van parked outside ——'

'A black or dark blue short-wheelbase Bedford van?' I asked.

He looked comically surprised.

'How the ——' then he nodded ruefully. 'So the police got that far, did they?'

'Yes. But I'm surprised they didn't connect your van ——'

He shook his head.

'Not mine. I hire vans from a chap up behind Baker Street. I had a virgin to deliver ——'

'A what?'

He smiled.

'An eighteenth-century French madonna in porphyry – curious piece – to a house in Bedfordshire. I often deliver sculptures myself to advise on siting and so on. She was lying in her packing case. I took out the virgin and put Maria in. Then I got the case into the van – not too difficult because there's a loading ramp. And then I went back to the party. And in the nick of time. I found Celia – my fiancée, you know – bearing down on the office.'

'But you were with her until the next morning. So how ——'

He shook his head again.

'No, I wasn't. She only thought I was. True, I was with her all evening. After the vernissage, I took her to Mewley's – do you know it? Good for game and that sort of thing. It's also good for wine and Celia does love claret. So I bought two bottles of it and when we got home she was a bit tiddly. Then I made love to her very thoroughly. And then she went to sleep and I knew that, after the claret and the love-making, she wouldn't wake up unless the house collapsed. So I got up and went back to the gallery and collected the van from the Mews, which is almost deserted at night, and drove off to Buttercups.'

'And why did you drop her where you did?'

He shrugged.

'Because I got lost. Simple as that. I'd intended to drop her in the woods outside Buttercups. I had a vague idea that it would look as if she'd been mixed up in some villainy there. But I just got lost and after driving around for half an hour or so looking for the right road, I realised I was running out of time. So I dropped her at the first isolated spot I came to. Then I drove back to the studio, parked the van outside, took a taxi most of the way home and was in bed again with Celia hours before she woke up.'

We were silent for a while, sipping our drinks. Then I said:

'The Superintendent – the one in Bristol – is a pretty tenacious fellow.'

He made a dismissive gesture.

'Oh, I suppose they'd have got me in the end. As a matter of fact, Celia's story wouldn't have held up for long. She'd got up in the night to have a pee. She asked me where I'd been in the morning and I told her down in the kitchen having a snack. It would have come back to her on a second or third interrogation. Then I have an idea there might be an old lady in Bradford who saw me shoot a rotten man. I don't underestimate the police.'

'So you've been expecting a visit from them?'

He smiled, a peculiarly charming smile.

'I was wondering who'd get here first – you or them. I'm rather glad it was you.'

'Why?'

'Kindred spirits. We're both freelances. And you're not a bad actor yourself, Mr Shoestring.'

It was a delicate question but one that needed asking.

'So your gun is here? In the flat?'

'That's right.'

'Would the police have found it?'

'I wonder? After each job I seal it professionally into a

genuine but minor work of art. Of course, I have to break and destroy the work of art to get it out – eats up a fair whack of the profits but I've considered it sound investment.'

I looked around at the profusion of ornaments.

'So it's in one of these, is it? Which one?'

'Guess.'

'Not my style. I'm a detective.'

He reached out for a delicate piece of porcelain that was standing on the small table beside his chair. It showed a gentleman in Regency costume kneeling beside a lady in Regency costume playing an instrument like a banjo for her. The only odd thing about it was that the gentleman was black – like Othello. It looked far too fragile to hold anything as brutal as an automatic. He held it up and contemplated it.

'Meissen,' he said. 'Pretty, isn't it?'

'And is the gun in there?'

'I wonder,' he murmured and dropped it. He reached quickly down and plucked something from the debris. 'Yes, it is,' he said delightedly, like a child who's found the treasure in a treasure-hunt.

He placed the weapon on the table where the Meissen group had stood. It was about two feet from his right hand and about ten from mine. There was no way I could reach it before he did. Other than by guile.

'Don't you think,' I asked persuasively, 'you've killed enough people?'

'No, I don't,' he said seriously. 'I think it's imperative that I kill one more.'

I must have tensed at that because the gun was in his hand when he added:

'Me, Mr Shoestring, not you.'

I relaxed again.

'With remissions ——' I began, but he made a disgusted noise.

'Really! You don't seriously think I'd spend the next fifteen years in prison, do you? I mean, what's the point? The Open University would be of no use to me because I'm

199

highly educated already. But, of course, that's not the essence, is it? The essence is that I've devoted myself to eliminating rotten men and there's one more who needs eliminating. I realise now what's wrong with killing swine. It kills the swine all right but it also creates killers. Why don't you go downstairs, Mr Shoestring? Then you can come back up and use the telephone.'

I cleared my throat.

'I hope it doesn't sound preposterously selfish ——' and a part of me laughed with self-mockery at how I was aping his style – 'but I can think of an objection to that scheme.'

'I won't try to escape.'

'No, it's not that. It's just – well, actually, I'm a suspect myself. It would certainly simplify things for me if you were still around to tell the police the whole story.'

'But they'll have enough evidence, God knows.' He gazed at me thoughtfully. 'Still, I can see your point. I'd be letting you in for a lot of aggro. All right.'

He put the gun down on the table beside him. Then he rose and went over to the drinks table. He was now much further from the gun that I was and I knew he was aware of the fact. I didn't move.

'The same?' he asked.

'Please.'

He made another round of drinks and returned with them.

'I suggest you phone the Yard now,' he said lightly.

I did so and the sergeant I spoke to promised, with civility and no sign of undue excitement, to despatch some men to the address I gave him immediately. While on the phone I refrained from looking at Mr Dixon. He was sitting near his automatic again and I felt a trifle queasy at the thought. But when I hung up, I found that he had risen and was pacing about the room. He said:

'I shall kill myself.'

'Oh?'

'Will you tell them I said that?'

'Well ——'

'I want you to. Then they'll have to take special

precautions – keep me under close observation. It will be a challenge. It always has been a challenge and it's appropriate that it should be for me too. But I'll make a statement first. You'll be in the clear, Mr Shoestring.'

'I'm grateful,' I said humbly.

We were still chatting cordially when the police arrived and arrested him.

It made the programme of the year. I told the whole thing soberly, playing down what I'd done. But I didn't need any false heroics. I knew and Don knew and the fans, once they'd heard the broadcast, knew that Eddie Shoestring had pulled it off. I'd brought in my man. And when I'd knocked on Dixon's door, I really had been laying my life on the line.

A week later, Erica said to me:

'You're a vain, egotistical pig.'

I glanced at the reporter from the *Sunday Record* to make sure he was out of earshot.

'But this is national publicity, Erica,' I urged reasonably. 'He's from a national paper.'

'National, regional, local – all you've done is give interviews for the past week.'

'Now, that's simply not true. I've taken on five new cases ——'

'Which is far more than you can handle. It just means you're greedy as well as being a vain, egotistical pig.'

'Could you lower your voice? Erica, I'm doing it for us.'

'Really? When did we decide that? I can't even recall being consulted.'

'You want that mansion, don't you?'

'No. I never did. You want it. I'm very happy with what used to be my own lovely home.'

'If that's a bitchy reference to the furniture ——'

'Oh, okay,' she admitted. 'You've replaced it – and the new stuff's very nice. It's just ——'

'Well, what?'

'You've changed, Eddie.'

'Well, of course I've changed. If I hadn't you could bury me. Everyone changes. It's called living.'

'No, I mean you've changed recently – since you've become a celebrity – and for the worse.'

'I'm not really a celebrity,' I asked modestly. 'Am I?'

'No,' she said furiously. 'You're a puffed-up little non-entity who thinks he is. All right, you're a nine-day wonder. Your investigation was very newsworthy. But it's not the whole of life. Eddie, don't sell out.'

'Okay,' I said, 'I won't.'

'I've seen practically nothing of you all week.'

'That's why we're going out to dinner this evening.'

'But we're not. You told me to meet you here at eight and here I am and you're going off with the reporter.'

'Only for an hour or so. Why don't you go up and have a drink with Don? He's still in his office and I'm sure he'll be delighted. Then, when I've given the interview, I'll collect you and we'll have a slap-up meal.'

'I'm going home.'

'What? Why?'

'I'll tell you why, Eddie. Just once. I'm not now – or ever – going to compete with the media for you.'

Then she smiled and took my hand. I glanced at Sonia who was watching with interest. The man from the *Sunday Record* was glancing at his watch. Erica said: 'Eddie, tell the reporter to go to hell. Come on – let's slip away – just you and me.'

'Gosh,' I said, with a lot of feeling in my voice. 'Don't I just wish I could? If you think this round of publicity and parties is any joy, you're crazy. But I've promised Don I'll do it for the station. He's never had it so good. And, after all, Erica, he's doubled my salary. We're going to be rich.'

She released my hand. 'How nice. Well, I'll just go back to the house and start digging.'

'Digging?' I asked, mystified.

'For the vault. Do you think the garden or the basement? I suppose we'll need electrified fences and guard dogs.'

'Erica, this is no time for sarcasm.'

'You know, I don't think I'll like you rich.'

'You never liked me poor.'

'But I loved you. See you, Eddie.'

And she turned and went out through the swinging doors of Radio West. I shook my head irritably and turned to the man from the *Sunday Record*.

'Right,' I said.

'Is there somewhere we can talk?' he asked.

'Certainly,' I said. I turned to Sonia. 'Anyone in the small studio?' I asked.

'No, Eddie,' she returned.

I led the reporter through to the small studio.

'So,' he said, when we were seated, 'why don't you tell it like it happened? At your own speed. You don't mind if I use the recorder?'

'Any mike's a friend of mine,' I assured him. 'Well, let's see, I first met Maria Calderes ——'

And the phone rang. I picked up the receiver irritably.

'Yes?'

'Think you'd better take this one, Eddie,' said Sonia.

I listened. There was a click and then a man's voice said:

'Mr Shoestring? Mr Raleigh here, assistant governor of Leadstone Prison.'

The familiar prickles started down my spine.

'Go ahead,' I said.

Dixon had been ingenious all right. He'd done it in the prison psychiatrist's office where he'd been interviewed daily while on remand. It was something to do with picking off the insulation on the wires running to the shrink's anglepoise lamp. Then, when the wires were bare, which had been this afternoon, he'd waited until the psychiatrist's attention was engaged, poured water over his hands from the psychiatrist's water-glass and electrocuted himself. Quick, neat, instantaneous.

'Thank you,' I said. 'Thank you for telling me.'

I hung up. A lot of things began to pass through my mind: a dead girl in a wood, a mindless man in a hospital, shot hoodlums, an electrocuted art gallery owner, a man trying to decide whether to be a monk or a father.

'Could you go on?' said the reporter. 'I have to catch a

train.'

I stood up.

'Catch it,' I said. 'Catch it. I've something to catch, too. Something that nearly got away.'

'But the interview? Aren't we going to do the interview?'

'No. Go find a celebrity to interview. I'm just a gumshoe. See you.'

And I walked hurriedly to the door and out.

When I reached the house, Erica was seated on the new sofa watching *Coronation Street*.

'You stay there,' I said. 'I'll make the dinner.'

'You'll what?'

'Thaw out a pizza.'

'What happened to your interview?'

'I axed it.'

'Why?'

'I had second thoughts. And they looked like you.'

'Oh, Eddie – I'm sorry. It's just ——'

'It's just that I've stood you up twice this week. And for what? Fame. And where does that lead? "The paths of glory lead but to the grave." Is that *Othello*?'

'No, it's Gray's Elegy.'

'Anyway, it's poetry. Like you.'

'Something's happened.'

'A million things. That's life. Every second, a million things happen. But you only meet Erica once.'

'This is a different Shoestring.'

'And a better one. Shall I thaw a pizza? Or shall we step out?'

Erica stood up. She looked me in the eye for a long time. She put her arms around my neck and kissed me. She said:

'Whichever you prefer.'

But in the end we did neither. We went upstairs to her bedroom instead.